Also by Ev Bishop

Bigger Things

Wedding Bands (River's Sigh B & B, Book 1)

Writing as Toni Sheridan

The Present

Drummer Boy

EV BISHOP

Ev Bishop (signature)

Hooked

River's Sigh B & B, Book 2

HOOKED
Book 2 in the River's Sigh B & B series
Copyright © 2015 Ev Bishop

Print Edition

Published by Winding Path Books

ISBN 978-0-9937617-7-5

Cover image: Kimberly Killion / The Killion Group Inc.

For my mom,
I miss you more than words can say.

And for my daughter,
I wish you could've known your maternal grandma.

And for my stepmom,
What a jumbled family we have! Thank you for your love.

Chapter 1

SAM WAS FRESH FROM THE shower, barefoot and dressed only in a robe. She wrapped her arms around herself and turned in a slow circle. Five stars or not, a hotel room was always just a hotel room, wasn't it? It was beautiful with its teak four-poster bed, matching highboy and desk, and snow-white linens, but generic nonetheless.

She settled into the leather wingback chair, the room's best feature in her opinion, and put her feet up. A niggle of surprise tickled her as she uncapped a pen and reached for her spiral bound notebook. Who'd have thought? Samantha Kendall using a *diary*. But she couldn't help it. The movement of her hand across page, the scent of the paper, the process of filling the sheet with the mess in her head—slowly at first, then so fast her hand cramped—soothed her and helped her see more clearly than she had in a long time. Her life, once so beautiful and busy, felt empty. Come to think of it maybe that was the appeal of the journaling. She filled something. Created a tangible mark that she was here. That she lived.

The coffee pot on the desk across the room sighed and sputtered.

"Ah, my faithful friend," she whispered, then got up, doctored herself a mug of the dark espresso blend, and settled down again.

She sipped her hot drink and drummed her fingers on her notebook. What to say, what to say?

She paused, drank more coffee, and ran her fingers through her damp hair. Finally she began to write.

Sheesh, three pages minimum is going to take hours today.

But it didn't. By the time she had two cups of caffeine in her, she'd churned out her minimum, plus another three pages—yet she wasn't calmed. She was edgier than ever. She scanned the last page, bit her lip and barely resisted the urge to tear the sheets loose and throw them away.

There's nothing I hate more than my sister being right about anything, but I have to hand it to Jo. She is right about this, and the pros and cons I wrote yesterday confirm it.

I always figured Aisha would reenter my life at some point, if only, like seems to be the case, for medical information and "closure." (How I hate that damn word!) I just thought I'd be at a spot in time, personally and pro-

fessionally, that I could be proud of—or at least not a bloody embarrassment. But at the same time, I guess it's not about me, is it? (Ha ha, quick, someone tell Jo I actually said that!) I would've done anything to have someone to talk to, when I was stuck in the same boat Aisha's in, so how can I refuse her request to meet?

My two biggest fears: that she'll ask about the asshole who fathered her. (What can I say about him that won't just be a huge ugly shadow over her?), or that she'll hate me—which is pretty hilarious because I definitely don't want her in my life permanently.

That was the line that stopped her. She shook her head, crossed the last line out, drew an arrow, and scribbled furiously.

That she'll hate me, which I'll totally understand, or worse, want something I don't have to give her. All of my love for her went out the door with her the day I gave her a chance for a better life. (Not that it seems to have panned out—but don't even get me started!) And what if she does want a relationship? I have no frigging clue what I'll do.

Samantha closed the book, and stashed it in her

suitcase.

She paid special attention to her outfit and did her makeup and hair just so, but it wasn't until she sprayed a light mist of perfume in front of her and walked through it that she admitted she'd made up her mind.

Yeah, yeah, yeah. She'd return to Greenridge. She'd see if she could be of any help to Aisha and answer any awkward questions her biological daughter had.

And then, so long as Jo and Callum were willing to let her monopolize one of their B & B cabins—and why wouldn't they? Her cash was as good as anyone's—she'd spend some concentrated time figuring out what exactly she wanted next and why her life, which she'd always enjoyed, wasn't enough for her these days.

She cocked her head, smiled at her reflection in the mirror, and nodded approval at both the image she projected and her new thoughts. She was an excellent planner and there was no reason she couldn't get herself back on track. And once she had a new direction, she'd leave Greenridge in the dust and never return. The place was a black hole. In lieu of a welcome sign at the beginning of town, there should be a plaque that read, "Abandon all hopes of having a life, ye who enter here."

And if Jo wanted to visit now and again? Well, she'd have to sojourn out of her hobbit village and head for the city. Sam was done with the ghost town of bad memories. She was sick of the family-focused "great place to raise kids" motto that everyone in town seemed to spout. Not everyone had kids or even wanted them. And she was beyond weary of how the place reminded her that except for her one solitary sibling, Jo, she had no family. Everyone was dead. There'd be no TV movie worthy reunion or redemption scene. Greenridge was like one big beer commercial for all the things she didn't have. And didn't want, she reminded herself.

Chapter 2

CHARLES TRIPPED OVER THE STUFFED-TO-BURSTING rucksack he'd stowed by his office door and stared at the ringing phone like it might bite. The call display showed T.C.O. Literary Management all too clearly, and unfortunately his agent Theresa, the "T" in T.C.O., knew he was home. After all, he'd just sent an e-mail seconds ago admitting it. He sighed heavily and picked up.

"Theresa, hi. Good to hear from you."

"Don't bullshit a bullshitter, and get real. You knew that e-mail wasn't going to fly."

"But—"

"And no buts." Her voice softened. "I feel for you. You know I do. And I'm on your side even if it doesn't feel like it, but it's time, Charlie. Past time. And if you can't see that, maybe it's time to rethink your career."

Charles sank into his office chair and rolled back and forth across the room. He didn't want to "rethink" his work. He loved what he did, what he wrote. Or he used to. And anyway, it wasn't like he hadn't considered doing something else. Just absolutely nothing came to him that didn't sink him even more deeply into the mire of apathy and disillusionment he seemed unable to pull himself from. And now, with Aisha living only God knew where and insisting she was staying there to have her baby, he didn't even have the occasional bright spot of her presence.

"You've used up all your reserve books, even your earliest ones that were previously unpublished for pretty good reasons. It's just a good thing some readers don't care what you write as long as the story says Jax Bailey on the cover."

"Thanks a lot."

"Oh, you know what I mean. Don't get pissy. I love your books. You've earned reader loyalty, but even diehard fans are starting to grumble on the Interwebs. You can only play the dead wife card for so long before people start to think you need to get over it."

Charles managed to not throw the phone across the room, but only just.

Theresa seemed to sense she'd crossed a line. "Sorry, that was crass. Obviously, healing isn't an easy one, two, three process. I know you're doing the best you can, just barely hanging on, and I know it will take time—but I'd hate to see you lose everything you worked so hard to build."

Too late. Everything he'd worked for died when Maureen did. Still, Theresa wasn't the enemy and she was on his side. He knew this. He also knew he'd probably exhausted every possible extension. He made a decent living, and Maureen's life insurance had paid off the mortgage and left a little besides, but not enough to see him through life—and definitely not enough to provide ongoing stability to Aisha and her little one, should she decide to keep it. And he was a young(ish) man still. Forty-four was nowhere near the time to retire even if it felt closer to eighty these days.

"They need a new book, or, and it's pretty nice of them, almost human in fact, they'll forgive the contract without penalty, but if you ever want to write for them again, it'll be like starting new."

Perish the thought—and no, that wasn't melodrama. "How long?" he asked.

"I got you six months, but that's it, final offer, last extension."

"Okay," he said.

"Okay?" Even though their connection was a little static-filled, the surprise in Theresa's voice was loud and clear. "Just like that you say *okay?*"

"Do I have a choice?"

"No, but I still thought you'd be a harder sell."

They wrapped the conversation up quickly from there, and Charles was careful to sound more positive than he felt. Six months, if he was his old self, was more than enough time to get a solid book to his publisher. But he wasn't his old self, and didn't think he ever would be again. Maureen had been gone three years, yet in some ways it was like she'd passed away yesterday, the grief would hit so fresh and raw. In other ways, however, it was like she'd left a lifetime ago, which, hard as it was, was sort of the truth. Neither his nor Aisha's lives were the same. They had new existences altogether, as if their time on earth had been divided into separate realities: Life with Mo. Life without her.

He stood up, scooted his chair under his desk and turned off his computer, then grabbed his laptop. He was sick of himself and the endless woe-to-me pool he wallowed in. Even his self-pitying thought about everything he'd worked for dying when Maureen did wasn't fully honest. Only half of what he worked for and lived for had passed on when she did. He still had their daughter, and who knows, maybe a grandbaby too.

He hit the lights and hefted his bag. Soon, with any luck, he'd be in a better writing space *and* headspace. For a moment he wondered if he should've told Theresa his plan, then shook his head. Where he spent his time wasn't her business and she'd just worry. Besides, though she'd be skeptical, he could write—or not write—just as easily in the boonies as he could at home.

And if Aisha was intent on setting up a temporary home in Greenridge, wherever that was, with this aunt whoever she was, in the hopes of connecting with her birth mom—who back in the day had seemed level-headed, but now he worried was a callous flake . . . well, he wasn't going to just abandon her to the wolves and wilds. He'd take up residence in one of the cabins that were "so far beyond cool that he couldn't possibly imagine how cool they were," to quote Aisha, and support her in whatever ways he could. She was the only family he had left, and if anything came between them, damaged their relationship, or hurt her, it would be over his dead body.

Chapter 3

SAM VEERED OFF THE HIGHWAY abruptly, and her Mercedes SUV skidded as it hit the soft shoulder. A wimpy horn sounded from the white Toyota traveling behind her and it crossed the centerline to give her room.

Sam flipped the driver the bird out of habit, but without a lot of heat. She had cut him off, after all. She caught a glimpse of surprised anger on the guy's face—he was cute, actually—then his own finger waved back in return.

When the small car whizzed past and rounded the bend out of sight, she was alone on the remote northern highway once more. She cut the engine and pressed clenched fists against her eyes. What was she doing? Why the hell was she heading back to Greenridge?

"It's the least you can do," Jo said in her head—except really she hadn't said that. No, her sister had been annoyingly mellow and pressure-free as usual, even though Aisha was still on the scene, hoping for some birth mother reunion special and sponging off Jo and Callum indefinitely, but at least until she had the baby. The *baby*. Sam wasn't even really a mother, and now she was going to be a grandmother?

"She'd like to meet you, yes," Jo's voice spoke again, this time from actual memory not projection. "But only because she wants to know if you regret giving her up or if you think you made the right choice. She's trying to decide what she should do."

"She should've kept her legs crossed from the get-go, that's what," Sam muttered, knowing her words were completely hypocritical but unable to stem them nonetheless.

"You don't have to come." Jo's voice again. "Aisha understands. She doesn't have any expectations."

It was that comment, about the lack of expectations, and her own stupid journaling that explained why Sam was in the middle of this godforsaken valley driving to the middle of nowhere. She understood all too well how many stacked-up disappointments it took to yield a "no expectations" approach to things, and from the little she'd heard about Aisha's life, she couldn't help but empathize. The least she could do was talk to the kid and answer her questions. She doubted she'd be much comfort or practical help, but for whatever it was worth, she could at least explain what the hopes behind giving her up had been—and let her know that she hadn't regretted it until she'd discovered that it hadn't worked out the way she had hoped.

12

She slowly raised her head, stretched her neck, and restarted the Mercedes.

Yes, she'd do what she'd come for, help the kid out the best she could with medical information and details about her own experience so she could make some sort of decision, and then she'd say good-bye. Again. Permanently.

SAM TOOK THE LONG DRIVEWAY too fast, then sprayed gravel in the parking area when she braked. She surveyed her surroundings briefly, before pulling off to one side of the main house. She had to give it to her little sister. The setting was breathtaking—if you liked to be surrounded by nothing but trees and mountains and water that is. Personally, she'd prefer a nice stretch of city sidewalk with fun high-end boutiques, the odd skyscraper or two, and a different restaurant to eat out at every night—but to each their own.

She eased out of the cream leather interior of her vehicle, contemplating whether she should wrangle her suitcases on her own or wait till she saw the cabin Jo was putting her in. Then she spotted something that made her breath catch.

Damn, damn, triple damn! That annoying little Toyota—she was sure it was the same one she'd cut off—was parked twenty paces away by a tiny bay-windowed cabin bearing a small sign that read "Rainbow" and sported a folk art styled fish.

Just her luck. The only person she'd annoyed on the road all day and it had to be someone bunking down at the same place she was staying. She sighed. Oh, well—maybe he wouldn't recognize her vehicle.

The door from the main house opened and Sam heard voices before she could see the people who went with them.

"Hey, that's the stupid overkill Mercedes that practically did a brake stand right in front of me on the highway," a low, masculine voice growled.

"Oh, crap," said Jo—very out of character language for her to use with a client.

Sam straightened her short skirt, smoothed her hair and walked out from the shelter of her ivory "overkill." *Pompous loser.* She held out her hand in greeting before she even cleared the vehicle. "So sorry about earlier—" she started to say, but the words stuttered to a stop.

When given more than a cursory glimpse at highway speed, the man in front of her was more than cute. Tall and lanky, with longish dark hair like some Victorian days' poet and a five o'clock shadow that made you want to run your hand along his jaw, he was gorgeous. But worse than that, he was *familiar.*

He gave her a foot to head perusal, but there was nothing flirtatious in his overt study—and no mutual recognition, just questions and condemnation. His eyes met hers.

Jo stepped off the porch that was hidden behind a copse of young pine trees, her mutt Hoover on her heels. Sam looked him over carefully, then petted him. She liked dogs okay, just not the things Jo's dog was famous for rolling in. "Sam, I wasn't expecting you so soon—but it's so good to see you. I can't wait to show you around—"

"Sam, as in Samantha Kendall, my daughter's biological mother?"

Sam winced and nodded.

Jo moved quickly and stood beside her. "I was so hoping Aisha would meet Sam first, but, well, she's not here at the moment and we are. Sam, this is Charles, Aisha's dad—Charlie, this is Sam."

"Aisha didn't say you'd be here." Charles said the word "you'd" like it was an insult and ignored Sam's outstretched hand. She dropped it quickly. What the heck was his problem?

Jo veered the conversation to more comfortable terrain—and Sam would've blessed her for it, except that she couldn't believe Jo hadn't given her a heads up and told her he was going to be there in the first place. "I'm sure there will be a lot of catching up to do, but you've both had long drives and like I said, I really think Aisha should get to meet Sam before, well, just before. . . . Charlie, you already have keys to your place."

Charlie grunted affirmation like a cave man. Sam managed not to roll her eyes. And he wasn't as good-looking as she'd initially thought—okay, no, he was, but he seemed like an ass and it was ruining his looks for her. What kind of deadbeat was he, and how had she so badly misjudged the profile letter the adoption agency had supplied all those years ago and thought he was good dad material?

Jo pulled an ornate key off a large ring and handed it to Sam. "We've put you in Silver. Breakfasts are, of course, included up at the main house every morning—and each cabin has a small kitchenette, but you probably haven't shopped yet, so if you want to join me and Callum for dinner tonight at our house, you're more than welcome."

"Will my daughter be there?"

Will my daughter be there? Sam mimicked Charlie's sour voice in her head, but listened for Jo's response with as much interest as he did.

"Yes." Jo grinned and tucked an errant blond curl out of her face. "She eats with us pretty regularly, and she's an amazing help around here, though I swear I try to get her to take it easy."

Charlie's face softened and he shook his head. "Aisha's never been one to do anything half way. If you got her to slow down and rest, eight months pregnant or not, well . . . I'd wonder what you'd done to her."

Jo laughed and Sam inched away, trying to be subtle. What was she doing here? She didn't belong. Not by any stretch of the imagination.

"She's a great kid. You and Mo did a wonderful

job raising her."

Sam almost snorted. If Jo was trying to reassure her or something, it wasn't working. This man and his deceased wife—sad story, but so what, who didn't have a sad story?—had failed Aisha. Sure, maybe it wasn't their fault. Death happened, whatever—but it wasn't Sam's plan. Her daughter was supposed to have everything she didn't have growing up, most importantly: two parents who loved each other and loved their child, who nurtured her and provided stability, raising her in one place, allowing friendships that endured, followed by educational opportunity—and instead she was knocked up at seventeen, living with an aunt and uncle she barely knew, in hole-the-ground Greenridge of all places. Her sacrifice had proven pointless. She could've raised a teenager that got knocked up in her senior year all by herself.

The similarities between Sam's own long ago situation and her offspring's were crushing and though she wasn't usually someone ever at a loss for words, she had none now. None at all.

The gravel crunched beneath her feet as she inched away, and she could just imagine the damage the sharp stones were doing to the stems of her Italian leather heels. Both Jo and the idiot shot her concerned looks.

"I'd love to join you, if you really don't mind." Charlie said, but his eyes were still on Sam.

"Great. We're eating at seven. Sam?"

Sam shook her head. "I'll give it a pass. Thanks

though. I'll see you for breakfast and make plans to speak with Aisha then. Please don't mention I'm here yet."

Jo's brow furrowed. "Are you sure?"

Sam nodded.

"Well, do you want . . . after dinner, can I come by your cabin to visit?"

"No, no, you're obviously busy. Are the other cabins full?"

Jo nodded and her happiness was so evident that Sam almost misted up. What was wrong with her? She crossed her arms and discreetly pinched the inside of her bicep until the overwrought emotional nonsense passed. "Well, I'm staying till I can't bear it another day, so don't sweat about making time for me. We'll have plenty of chances to chat—now do you have someone who carries a person's bags, or do I have to do it myself?"

"Er, normally, guests carry their own gear, but I can help."

"No, you're cooking dinner. I'll do it." Charlie strode toward the SUV.

Sam practically sprinted to catch up—quite a feat in her heels on the blasted gravel. "Not necessary. I was just asking."

"It's no problem, and, well"—Charlie's gaze dropped to her feet—"you're not exactly dressed practically for carrying anything very heavy."

If the condescending jerk thought Sam would apologize for not dressing like some mountain person, he had another thing coming. She waited until his eyes finally lifted to meet hers again—and observed his irises were a dark chocolate brown, something she usually found quite attractive. "Fine," she said coolly. "I have two suitcases and a carry on." She clicked the trunk release on her key fob. The Mercedes beeped once and its back door lifted slightly.

Without looking back or making any false noises of appreciation—meddler!—she strode toward the cabin identified as "Silver" by a small sign similar to the one that marked Charlie's "Rainbow." It too featured a bay window on one side and a covered deck off the front door. Very cute.

She turned to check her concierge's—ha ha— progress with her bags, and was surprised to find him so close behind her that she almost smacked into his chest. She moved right and paused, momentarily sidetracked by the view, despite herself: a lush forest with soft, pine-needled paths winding this way and that. And the best part? Rainbow cabin, where Charles was booked, was nowhere in sight, due to a trio of massive cedar trees—at least she thought they were cedar; they smelled good anyway.

She shivered a little. On one hand, it was super cool how instantly private and secluded the cabin was after such a short walk. On the other, it was kind of creepy. She might as well be alone in the woods with this cretin—if you could fairly call someone a cretin just for volunteering to carry your bags for you, unasked. She unlocked the door without speaking, flicked on a light switch, and stepped into the main room.

"Wow, nice digs," Charlie said, following her in and setting her suitcases down.

"Nice" was an understatement. All natural wood and stone and glass, with a ceiling that was pretty much all sky light, every surface and item in the place was a treat for the senses, calling to be touched or rested upon. A buttery leather loveseat beckoned, and Sam smiled when she saw the array of chocolate Jo had set out on the nearby coffee table.

"That table is killer," Charlie said, slipping out of his shoes and padding over to it for a closer look.

Killer? What was he? Twelve? Sam thought. But it was amazing, he was right about that. Constructed from the inverted root ball of some ancient tree, the thing was a work of art.

"Is Rainbow like this?" Sam asked, a thread of worry weaving through her. If this was the standard of all the cabins, how deeply in debt had Jo and Callum jumped?

Charlie shook his head. "Not even close—comfortable enough, but rustic. Definitely rustic." He looked down at his shoeless feet and froze. "Uh, I'm sorry—kind of weird of me to make myself at home in your place."

Sam waved the words away. "No apology needed.

Let's check out the shower together."

He turned an adorable shade of bright red, which, to her shock, triggered a flood of heat to her face too. "I just meant . . .'cause I bet it'll be fancy too."

And it was. It *really* was. So fancy, in fact, it would rival any deluxe spa. Floor to ceiling windows showcased a stunning view of a rushing creek against a backdrop of evergreens and birch that would bud soon but for now were just pretty silver arms stretching into the sky.

The view would've more than made up for even the simplest of utilities—a sole washbasin would've sufficed. But no, the room boasted a Japanese soaker tub, an infrared sauna, and a glass-encased two-person massaging shower. The vanity was a swath of ebony wood that seemed to magically support itself along one wall, with a heavy ceramic bowl and a simple swan-necked faucet for a sink.

Sam stroked the counter with appreciation and turned to Charlie. "Can you believe this place? It's crazy!"

Charlie met her eyes again, opened his mouth—then shut it without saying anything. Weirdo. She shrugged, a little disappointed that he didn't seem as impressed as she was, but then why would he be? He was a stranger and had no idea how much joy bringing this all together would have brought Jo—and Sam was no dummy. Jo had created this space with her, Sam, in mind. "Silver" indeed. She'd better be charging her a pretty penny for it, no discount.

She left the bathroom and strode back to the entranceway. "Thank you for carrying my bags in. I'm sorry I was rude," she said at the exact same time Charles said, "I'm sorry if I was pushy."

They both broke off speaking.

Sam surprised herself by smiling. Maybe she and this awkward man had something in common, after all—besides Aisha, that is.

Just as the tiny positive thought sparked, however, the dunce squashed it. "So when are you leaving? If you change your mind about needing to see Aisha, I'd be happy to give her a message from you."

Sam opened the door with too much force and practically shoved Charles onto the porch. She didn't "need" to see Aisha. Aisha wanted to see her, and if Charlie thought easing his own discomfort at having the birth mom around was more important than what his young, pregnant daughter needed, well—he could stuff himself. It only made her more determined to see what help she could be to Aisha, then to get the hell out of dodge.

Chapter 4

CHARLES PUSHED HIS CHAIR BACK from the table and stretched his legs out. He hadn't eaten like that in . . . well, he had no idea how long. He took in the happy faces around him.

Aisha was, cliché or not, glowing. Her baby bump was like a basketball shoved up her sweatshirt. She didn't look pregnant. She looked like a kid playing a joke.

Jo was great, and though it hurt a bit, he totally understood why his baby girl felt connected to her aunt. They were practically clones, appearance-wise—and from the laughter and smiles of the other two guests from Sockeye cabin, Jo made everyone at the table, not just him, feel like she'd always known them.

Callum, Jo's husband, looked more like some business tycoon than the mastermind behind the mindblowing dessert they'd just enjoyed, some multilayered chocolate, caramel and cream thing that defied description—exactly as Aisha had promised it would, "even for a word nerd like him."

But sharp, miss-nothing gaze aside, Callum seemed friendly and laid back. He followed Jo's every movement with appreciative eyes, obviously a man still smitten.

When Callum got up to help Jo clear the table and bring coffee to him and the other guests, Charlie's heart panged. Even after three years, the loss of all the little things he'd always taken for granted were what ached the most. Who'd ever know that things like not having someone to clear the table with, or to rock-paper-scissor battle about taking out the trash, would throb like an infected sliver, long after your spouse was gone? People recognized the bigger elements of grief and tried to prepare you—as if anything could—but it was the tiny details that sliced like knives, causing small emotional bleeds when he least expected it. He welcomed the pain of remembering, though, because sometimes he worried the sharpness of missing Maureen was fading, that he was forgetting, and that would be worse.

"I swear you guys are trying to kill me, but thank you," Charlie said as Callum set down a small pitcher of warmed cream for the coffee.

Callum slapped Charlie's back. "That's what *I* always say to Jo—but die happy, right?"

The table laughed and a lump formed at the back of Charlie's throat, choking him. How he prayed his love for Mo had been as obvious to her as Callum's must be to Jo. Aisha reached for his hand beneath the table and squeezed it hard. He looked over at his daughter, but she didn't turn toward him.

"And as I always say," Jo quipped, "no dying, happy, sad or otherwise, till the dishes are done."

Everyone laughed again and Charlie returned Aisha's hand-squeeze and wished he could offer her even a smidgeon of what she'd found in this loud, all-welcoming place. He hadn't even spent the night at River's Sigh and he was already hooked.

His thoughts flitted to Sam, alone in her cabin. Why hadn't she joined them for dinner? In some ways it made sense. She probably wanted her and Aisha's first introduction to be more private, less casual . . . but then again, who, with insider access to all this, wouldn't want to take part?

Aisha interrupted his contemplation. "Friday and Saturday nights anyone who wants to can come for dinner, overnight guests or people from town, you name it—and the price for what you get is so cheap."

"Even if it was a hundred bucks a head, it'd be worth it." His response seemed to make her happy. She beamed, then hopped up effortlessly, like she wasn't carrying an extra forty pounds smack dab in her middle. "I'll clean up, Jo."

"No, no—you've done enough. Rest and visit your dad."

"I insist."

Charlie stood up. "I'll be her lackey. She can point to things and tell me what to do. It'll be a win-win. I'll get to visit her and she'll avoid taking it easy at all costs."

The Sockeye guests said happy-sounding good-nights, Jo acquiesced to Aisha and Charlie's demand to let them help, and Callum tugged Jo away.

Clean up went quick and fast, showing Aisha really was a regular feature at the main house for meals. All too soon, she'd pecked his cheek, wished him good-night and headed off to bed herself.

Charlie left the cozy warmth of the main house for the cool, wet darkness of the outdoors, torn between gratitude and sorrow. It was wonderful to see Aisha thriving and more at peace than she'd been in months, maybe even in years, since Mo died. But it was brutal too. He would lose her to her new biological family. How could he not?

It wasn't late, maybe ten or so, and he knew he should get some words in because that was the new plan: new words every day, regardless of how late it got, before he let himself hit the sack. Despite all that fresh resolve, however, he found himself turning the opposite way of Rainbow, planning to walk a bit, check out the other cabins, and stir up his creative juices. Or that was the excuse for tonight's procrastination anyway.

He'd forgotten that Sam's cabin was the first one he'd come to. Instantly he was irritated. There was just something about her that set him off, put him on edge. She was so . . .

Hot.

The word jumped into his brain and made him slam his fist against his palm in denial. She was not hot—and if she was, it was irrelevant. She was Aisha's birth mother, a critical part of the huge extended family trying, however unintentionally, to steal *his* family.

And besides, she wasn't his type. She was the opposite of low key, down-to-earth, practical Mo in every way.

Plus he hadn't looked at another woman in over twenty years; he wasn't starting now. Still—it would be nice if he could manage not to be a douche canoe every time he saw her. He slapped a hand to his forehead. Douche canoe? That was as bad as when he'd said "nice digs" and "killer" earlier. Just because his kid talked in some strange cross of 50s gangster and modern-hipster-weirdo, didn't mean he should.

A small light inside Silver cabin flickered and Charlie realized it was a candle. Sam was in there all alone, probably hungry having eaten nothing but sweets for dinner, and he'd usurped her place at her sister's table.

Then again, being alone in that space, maybe taking a soak in that bathroom, chocolate and wine close at hand, might not be torture after all.

A hunger that had nothing to do with a desire for food rumbled through him—so strong, so unfamiliar and so unexpected he almost tripped. And that would be perfect, right? To fall down, make a racket, then have to explain why he was standing outside her door in the middle of the night, staring at her darkened windows, fantasizing about her lounging around in that steamy tub—okay, so he wouldn't actually have to mention that last part, but that was what he was doing, wasn't it?

He'd been standing so close to her earlier that he'd been able to smell her, all expensive perfume and product, yes, but earthy and sensual ones, like he'd imagine a hippy-turned-yuppie might wear. And those high heels. Weren't rounded toe, thick-rubbered shoes the feminine footwear of choice in these here parts? She was in the middle of the bush in northern British Columbia, for crying out loud, yet she was dressed like the heroines from his books. And not only had he noticed her—the first female to register with him in forever—but his body *liked* noticing her.

His blood thundered in his ears as, incredibly un-helpfully, a vision of her in those stupid shoes slid into his mind. He remembered how she'd caressed the bathroom's luxurious counter with such obvious pleasure, then imagined her bending to turn on the hot water to fill the tub. The room was misty when she motioned him closer. "Will you?" she purred—

Except wait, it wasn't a purr. It was a cold, abso-lutely real, not-a-chance-in-hell-it-was-only-his-imagination voice. And it was right behind him. "Will you, please," the voice repeated, "tell me what the hell you're doing?"

The steam in his mind chilled and dripped icy embarrassment down his spine. "I, er, was just out walking off dinner."

Sam stepped into the ring of light thrown by a solitary bulb mounted on a pole in the center of the parking area. "No, *I* was out walking. *You* are standing by my porch, gawking at my cabin like a stalker."

Rats. Exactly what he'd been scared he'd look like.

"Should I be worried?" she continued.

He shook his head, one hundred percent flustered yet again—and made the poor choice of glancing down. The high heels and silky-looking expanse of bare legs were gone, but what he saw was no less disarming. Figure-caressing black leggings, with slouchy suede leather boots. A light drizzle started and he latched onto that inane fact as a much welcomed distraction. "I hope you sprayed weather protector on those things."

One of Sam's eyebrows shot up. She pulled her knit wrap tighter around herself. "Rainbow cabin is that way," she said, speaking slowly and enunciating carefully, like she was talking to a dunce—something that was more than fair, he figured. "Get lost."

Thankful for the dark that would hopefully conceal yet another flush of embarrassment, Charles obeyed, taking long, easy strides to hide how he felt: that he was slinking away in shame.

THE TUB WAS EVERY BIT as glorious as Sam had imagined it would be. She stretched out in the mango-scented water, made a mental note to tell Jo what a nice treat the bath products were, and sipped her wine. A glass in and she was a little lightheaded already, not typical for her at all, but what could she say? Maybe a bar of dark chocolate, though delicious, wasn't the best dinner.

The creek and trees beyond the window were a soft black blur, but above that darkness, the sky was a plush navy, sprinkled heavily with bright stars. It was like a scene out of a movie, so beautiful it made you bittersweet.

Sam sighed. Tomorrow was another day, as ol' Scarlet would say, but for tonight, at least, Sam was glad she'd come. Excited for Jo. And sure it was the perfect space to screw her own head on right again. She was also happy it appeared that Jo and Charles had honored her request and hadn't told Aisha she was here yet. It would be better to meet fresh in the morning, then they could stamp out some boundaries, decide when to chat—

A glimmer of movement low to the ground outside the closest window interrupted Sam's planning. She leaned forward, water sloshing, and peered into the thick night. A little shiver coursed down her spine. Great, the place was surrounded with wild animals. Either that or she'd just given one of Jo's staff a big eyeful.

She'd assumed the luxurious windows were privacy glass, but maybe she should've confirmed it. Then again, if there was someone out there, who cared? They could enjoy the show. It was pretty tame anyway: "Lonely woman gets drunk having a solo soak." But she couldn't really feel sorry for herself. Not tonight. Not here. She sipped again and relaxed lower into the water once more. She loved that the tub had a heating element so your water never cooled. To heck with the rest of Silver cabin. She might just spend all her time submerged.

She started on a third glass of wine, her buzz less noticeable now, and thought back to catching Charles staring at her cabin. She was used to men either loving her, or finding her attractive anyway, or hating her, pretty much on sight. Charles definitely fit into the second category, probably because he incorrectly viewed her as some threat to his daughter's affections or wellbeing. She'd set his mind at ease. Eventually. For now it would be fun to let him stew a bit.

She did wonder why he'd stood outside her cabin so long, though. It was almost like he was trying to screw up courage to do something—maybe to knock on her door. If he wasn't such a jerk, wouldn't it have been fun if what he'd actually wanted was to check out the shower together, like *really* together?

Another little shiver coursed through her—and this one had nothing to with the difference between the air temperature and her lovely steamy water. She sipped more wine and rubbed her right foot over her left one. He had seemed taken with her legs—or weirdly concerned about her choice of footwear and ability to protect it from the elements, anyway. For this fantasy she'd go with the former. . . .

No. She sat up abruptly. She was not going to wet dream about that man. Greenridge, as she knew all too well from the months spent with Jo settling their Uncle Ray's estate, had a complete shortage of appropriate men to play around with, true. But that said, she shouldn't get all mushy minded about Charles. It would be weird. Weird and pathetic. He was her biological child's adopted father, for crying out loud. Widowed or not, it made him seem *taken*. And people could say what they wanted about her, but even in her fantasy life, Sam wasn't someone to mess with taken men. Except that one time all those years ago, and look how that turned out: a surprise pregnancy—and an even bigger surprise that the man she'd hung all her hopes on didn't give a shit about pretty-but-naïve-as-hell Samantha Kendall.

Ah well, hindsight was twenty-twenty and all that, and anything her childhood hadn't taught her, Rick certainly had. When they'd met, his smooth tongue and flattery easily convinced the lonely kid she'd been that maybe there were such things as true love and soul mates, despite her mother's pathetic track record with a long line of losers. What could she say? She used to be stupid, but she'd been wised up for a long time now.

Sam set her glass down heavily beside the now-finished wine bottle and closed her eyes. Why was she thinking on those painful, humiliating ancient days? Well, because the primary evidence of her stupidity was back in her life, of course. And what on earth should she tell young Aisha about her conception? She'd like to get away without having to tell her anything at all.

Chapter 5

DAMN, DAMN, TRIPLE DAMN. SHE should've asked Jo what time breakfast started so she could've been early, one of the people watching other folks' grand entrances instead of the reverse. Even from out on the porch she could see the dining room was packed. Where did all the people come from? It wasn't like River's Sigh B & B was a high capacity venue. The house's windows glowed a cheery welcome in the damp, foggy morning, but all Sam wanted to do was turn and flee.

This place, this situation, isn't me, she thought. Yet she turned the door handle and stepped into the steamy room regardless. It was filled with noisy laughter and chat—far too energetic for morning, if you asked her— and the stomach-rumble-inducing aromas of bacon, cinnamon, and coffee.

As she neared the table, all sound stopped and every eye in the place turned toward her. She almost bolted, but then Jo was there.

"Hey, Sam. Help yourself. And everybody? This is my sister Sam. Sam, this is everybody."

Samantha nodded and returned the collective smiles, then, thankfully, was forgotten and conversations resumed.

Sam was ravenous, but with the exception of chocolate and alcohol, she pretty much avoided all refined carbs—so she contented herself with one deep, lingering inhale near a platter of huge cinnamon buns oozing brown sugar and cream cheese drizzle, then armed herself with a plate of two eggs over easy, four strips of bacon, and a mug of caffeine.

She scanned the table. It was beyond pathetic that aside from Jo, who was understandably too busy to sit, the only person she remotely knew was Charles. He glanced up as she approached, then quickly directed his gaze elsewhere. Fine. She didn't want to sit with a guy that drove a Toyota anymore than he wanted to sit with her. Okay, actually she could care less about the Toyota, but if he was going to snub her for no good reason, she was going to return the favor in spades. She settled at the end of the table furthest away from everyone, and noted, just for the record, not because she cared, that there was no one young or pregnant present.

She ate her eggs first because both coffee and bacon were equally delicious at any temperature, and did a quick inventory.

Herself, eating alone.

Jo, buzzing guest to guest like a manic butterfly crossed with a good fairy.

Someone clanking away in the kitchen just out of sight—Callum, she assumed—who was no doubt, according to every Callum fact Jo continually burdened her with, the person guilty of creating those cinnamon buns she wasn't having.

Two older women, apparently also avoiding carbs, eating scrambled eggs that looked yolkless. Shit, was that her future? Holidays with spinster friends, no one enjoying decadent foods in case their waists, heaven forbid, expand an inch? No, not likely her fate. She didn't have any female friends.

Two men, too young for her—never her thing at all—so not really notable, except that one was loudly cataloging all the work he had to do around the place. Note to self, she thought. Give Jo and Callum a heads up that staff should be informed that employees *work*, that's their whole raison d'être, so monologues about duties are out of place, especially when fortunate enough to be welcomed for breakfast before their shift.

Charles. Absorbed in the cinnamon bun he was devouring. Lucky jerk.

Another woman, about her age, who smiled and murmured good-morning when Sam glanced over. Sam started to return the greeting, but a bearded man came up behind the woman, bent and kissed her cheek. Sam was understandably forgotten.

So . . . a couple employees, the cabins' other occupants, definitely no Aisha.

Jo appeared at her side and plunked into the chair

to Sam's right. "Whew," she said, helping herself to Sam's last piece of bacon. "No rest for the wicked."

"Yeah, I guess, but I'm not tired."

"Heh." Jo grinned. "Can I grab you anything else? More bacon perhaps?"

"Hmm, maybe one more slice? It kinda feels like I shorted myself or something."

Jo laughed, got up and returned a moment later, with six more slices of bacon, a plate of orange wedges, and a carafe of coffee.

"You know, keep this up, and I might never leave."

"That's what I'm hoping."

Sam held up her hand. "Don't go getting all crazy. I just meant I really appreciate how you're spoiling me. It's a great place, Jo. I mean it—and how much are you gauging me for Silver, by the way?"

"For you? Don't be silly. Callum and I have already discussed it. No charge. We're using you to break in the service. You can just give us pointers—"

"Not a chance. I won't even accept a discount," Sam interrupted.

"Come on—"

"No."

"Fine. We'll fight about it later."

They munched bacon in silence for a moment, then Jo said, "It's really good to see you again, to have you back so soon. I mean it."

"You're acting like you don't know the only reason I'm here."

The two older women at the far end of the table stood up. "Thank you so much," they called in unison and one added, "Delicious, yet again."

Jo waved and then said good-bye to the woman with the bearded man as they left too. The young bucks had apparently decided to work instead of just talk about working and shuffled out after the paying guests. It was down to Callum, still clanking in the kitchen, Charles—who she'd covertly noticed was on his second sticky bun—and her.

"Is she avoiding me?" Sam asked softly, playing with an orange rind.

Jo looked surprised, then apologetic. "No, not at all. She just has your sleep genes. She's a great worker, like I've said, but I've yet to see her awake before eleven. I should've told you that when you mentioned waiting till breakfast to make plans. I didn't even think."

Sam shrugged. "No worries."

"I'm pretty busy until one, but then things simmer down. I was thinking we could have tea here, say two-ish? I'll introduce you guys and then you can cue me. If you want me to stay, I will. If you're more comfortable talking to her alone, I'll take off."

A cough sounded from the other end of the table. Sam looked over. Charlie nodded, not even having the decency to pretend he hadn't been eavesdropping and now apparently with some mistaken notion he should be a part of this conversation.

"I think," he said, proving her right, "you and I should talk before you and Aisha meet."

Sam crossed her arms over her chest, then uncrossed them. "And why's that?"

"My daughter, I mean Aisha—"

"I know who she is. Just call her Aisha."

"Fine." Charles got up, walked the length of the room, and sat across from Sam.

Jo cleared her throat, but topped up her coffee without saying anything.

"Aisha," he finally spoke again, "is really vulnerable right now. She comes across as super confident, tough even, but she's actually a tender soul. It hurt her a lot when her mom died, and while I did the best I could, I probably wasn't—no, for sure I wasn't—as much help or support as I should've been."

Sam crossed her arms again, and this time they stayed that way.

"I know it must be tough," Jo said, "but what exactly are you trying to say?"

"I don't want Samantha to meet her," he answered Jo, then fixed his eyes on Sam. "She doesn't need you. She had a mother, a perfect, amazing, wonderful mother. You can only disappoint her." His words poured in a torrent and he looked a little horrified by them. "I'm sorry. That came out badly. I just mean—"

"That you think I'll somehow be a disappointment? No, that was loud and clear—and I guess we're even-Steven because I was pretty disappointed myself to find you raised the kid to the same pathetically low standard I could've managed on my own."

"Sam, stop it."

"No, you stop it, Jo. We're all grown ups here and as Chuck so eloquently pointed out, perhaps he and I *should* talk before Aisha and I meet. I'm not the one who searched for her. I'm not the one who requested, not once, not twice, but multiple times that I please talk with her."

"Sam . . . " Jo said.

"Come on," Charles sputtered.

Sam shook her head. "Like it or not, Aisha wants me in her life, and that means, whether you like it or not, I will be—at least to answer any questions she has."

"You don't understand. I didn't mean . . . I wasn't saying what it sounded like—I just don't want her hurt again. She makes attachments easily but feels them strongly when they break apart. She lost her mom. The father of her baby is a total loser. You didn't—for good reasons, admirable reasons, reasons I'll always be grateful for—want to keep her, so please don't waltz in and out now. It's just easier if you don't become part of her life."

Sam jumped to her feet, a livewire of rage sparking through her. She tried to kindle the fury even hotter—how ignorant he was, how condescending, how holier-than-thou—in a desperate hope that the anger would mask the insecurity flooding through her. Because he was right. She had had the best of reasons to give her baby up, and all those reasons were still applicable. And she had been planning a quick Q and A and a fast exit, all very smooth and neat—how had he known? And would that be damaging to Aisha, or was it all she needed? Jo said the girl had no expectations, just wanted information.

Unfortunately the words she mustered were neither as angry nor as confrontational as she wanted them to be. "Who would that really be easier for, Chuck? You, me or Aisha?"

"Stop calling me Chuck," Charles whispered, his tone seething—a completely asinine response in Sam's opinion.

The phone rang, making them all jump. Jo waved it away. "The machine will get it." She shook her head. "I'm sorry you guys both ended up here at the same time. It makes it harder than it already is—" Both Sam and Charles started to object, but Jo spoke over them. "I know Aisha feels badly that you feel hurt by all this, Charles—but she really does want to meet Sam. She isn't a legal adult, true, but she is seventeen and she's going to be a parent herself any day. Not letting her make her own decision about this seems wrong."

Charles glared, eyes narrowed, jaw tight.

Sam nodded, but inside she still wasn't sure. Maybe Charles was right. She bit her lip—and the bullet. "Look, for what it's worth, whatever you're afraid of, I'll do my best to support Aisha too. I only ever

wanted the best for her, and about the crap I just said—
"

"I'm not *afraid* of anything," Charles growled. Sam's anger flared again.

Jo started to say something else, but a flurry of activity stopped her. Callum jogged into the room. On his heels came a worried-looking girl with a mop of blond curls pinned up with chopsticks. The stress on her face intensified as she looked from Charles to Sam to Jo.

Aisha, Sam thought, knowing the Jo-look-alike couldn't be anyone else. She could only stare. She was . . . beautiful. Not quite as tall as she was, more compact—again like Jo—but plumper, no doubt because of the pregnancy. Green eyes just like her own, though—and just as Sam rubbed at the ring she wore on her right hand with her thumb, the girl did the exact same thing to a ring she wore. Was there a genetic code for nervous tells?

Aisha locked gazes with Sam who was still standing a few paces behind Jo, and recognition seemed to hit her too. Her mouth fell open. Before anyone could respond to Aisha's obvious surprise, however, Callum spoke in a low, tense voice. "Ah, Jo? Can I steal you a minute? We have a problem."

Chapter 6

CHARLES WAS AT AISHA'S SIDE in a heartbeat, taking her arm in case she was in danger of falling. "What, what is it? What's wrong?"

Aisha shook loose of his grasp. "God, Dad—it's not me. I'm fine."

Charles stepped back uneasily.

"The kid's fine," Callum affirmed and turned toward Jo again. "But the bookings are not."

Aisha darted another glance at Sam, as if torn—but something, responsibility maybe, or nerves, won out. "I'm so sorry," she wailed. "It's all my fault."

Good grief, Charlie thought, wasn't Sam going to formally introduce herself? What was she thinking?

Jo was up from the table and moving toward Callum. "What's wrong with the bookings?"

Callum's mouth opened, but it was Aisha who spoke first. "You told us not to book Silver, that you wanted it held because you knew, uh . . . "

"That Sam, your birth mom, was coming. Right—oh, *right*. Shoot." Jo motioned toward Aisha and Aisha

43

let herself be led over to Sam. "I'm sorry it's in the middle of some crisis, but let me introduce you guys. Sam, meet Aisha. Aisha, this is—"

"Sam," Sam said, holding out her hand. It trembled a little and Charlie wondered if Aisha noticed too.

"I'm sorry to take away from the big moment," Callum interrupted, "but we really have to deal with this."

Aisha broke contact with Sam, almost like she was relieved to have something else to focus on. "Yeah, sorry. Like I said, I knew she, Sam, was coming, but I didn't know when or I forgot, and I was so excited because at two hundred bucks a night—"

Jo held up a hand. "It doesn't matter who booked it or why. When's the conflict?"

Callum and Aisha exchanged anguished looks.

"When?" Jo repeated.

Charles shifted uncomfortably, watching their non-verbal communication. Jo, Callum, and Aisha—they already related in a completely familiar, family-esque way. Almost unconsciously, his gaze brushed over Sam. She looked as tortured and out of the loop as he felt. For a split second he thought, Sam's like me, she's my ally—then common sense overwrote his wishful thinking. He was alone. In a battle not to lose his only child—and sole living link he had to his wife—to the ridiculously, apparently perfect family. Things were awkward between Sam and Aisha right now, but they wouldn't always be and then that'd be that.

"Today," Aisha said. "But they arranged it last week."

Callum winced. "Yeah, they know check in time is three p.m., and they just called to say they'd be arriving a little late, sometime after eleven tonight, and wanted to make sure we held the room and to confirm there'd be someone here to meet them, give them keys, etc. Aisha didn't tell them it was already occupied. She just said she'd find out what the procedure was for late arrivals and we'd get right back to them."

For a moment the room was absolutely silent.

"We booked them in *advance,* and they're expecting Silver cabin *tonight*?" Jo's voice was steady, but her tightly clasped hands revealed her stress.

"Sorry, hon." Callum winced again.

"I'm sorry too." Aisha full on grimaced.

"It's okay." Jo scrubbed her face with both hands. "There's an easy solution. We'll just have to apologize, explain there was a double booking, and eat a little crow. I'll call around and find another room for them, somewhere in town—"

"You're right," Samantha said, stepping out from behind Jo. "There is an easy solution, but not the one you're suggesting."

"So what then?" Jo asked while Callum and Aisha stared hopefully.

"Well, it's definitely not giving away your booking and burning bridges with a new-to-you customer," Sam said. "I'll move on. No worries. And the room's very clean. It won't take a lot housekeeping-wise to get it ready for someone else."

"No." Jo's brow furrowed. "You just got here."

"I'm sure we can think of something else. You don't need to leave," Callum said.

"Wait, say what?" Aisha's voice was a touch shrill. "We've barely met, and you're already taking off?"

Charlie reacted to the pain in Aisha's tone without properly thinking it through. "No one's going anywhere. I have two bedrooms. Sam can stay with me." Every head in the room turned toward him.

Jo shook her head. "Absolutely not. Sam's a paying guest. She won't even let me give her a discount—and Silver's the type of room she would book. Rainbow isn't her style at all."

"But Rainbow's amazing. So what if it's not ritzy? It's not like it's a dump or anything." Aisha gave Sam a withering glare like she, not Jo, had been the one to imply Rainbow was somehow beneath her, and Charlie almost felt sorry for her—then steeled himself against that emotion. Sam *had* been thrilled by the opulence of Silver, and she dressed like a princess, sat apart from everyone at breakfast. . . . It was good for Aisha to see her as the aloof, cash-conscious diva she obviously was. Aisha could ask whatever questions she had that Charlie couldn't answer, and then she and he could move on with their lives and let Samantha Kendall move on with hers, the way she'd planned to right from the time she'd given birth.

Jo took a deep breath, Aisha looked like she was holding in further biting comments, and Callum waved the cordless phone. "Aisha said we'd call right back. What should I say?"

Sam rolled her eyes. "That the room is theirs, of course. You guys aren't allowed to do anything that might hurt business or cause bad word of mouth on my account. They'll love Silver and rave about it to everyone they know—exactly what you need. You don't need to woo me. You already know I'll be a repeat visitor. Maybe anyway."

Jo sighed and nodded, Callum headed out of the room to make his call, and Sam's gaze rested on Charlie.

Like a moron he felt himself blush. Again. You'd think he'd never seen a woman before. "I appreciate the offer, Charles, but thanks but no thanks. I'll take a place in town. The set up here's already a little too cozy for me."

Charlie nodded, and Sam turned to Aisha. "I'm sorry our first meeting wasn't a little more special or something."

Aisha shrugged.

"And please don't think by not staying at Rainbow I'm somehow criticizing it. I'm sure the cabin's grand. I just have personal space issues. We'll connect though. Don't worry. Let me get settled, and we'll make a coffee date."

Aisha studied Sam's face for a long moment and

Charlie, knowing how the scrutiny of the young felt, wondered how Sam was taking it. "That'd be great," Aisha finally said softly. "I . . . appreciate it."

Sam nodded and cleared her throat. "Of course. No problem."

"Are you really sure you don't mind?" Jo's tone said she wasn't happy with the solution, no matter that Sam suggested it or not.

Sam stepped back from the group again, yet her smile remained warm enough. She was hard to read, Charlie thought. Very hard. "One hundred percent," she said.

"I'll start calling around for you."

"Don't be silly. I'll take care of it."

"Are you sure?"

"God, Jo. Enough already." Sam strode across the room, but stopped and turned at the doorway. "I am going to miss that gorgeous tub though. I think I spent all night in it."

Sam's eyes met Charlie's, almost like she was, what? Directing the bathtub comment at him? Flirting? He wished.

Jo smiled. "I thought you'd like it."

Sam left and the room felt really big with just him, Jo and Aisha in it.

"So what are your plans today?" Jo asked.

"I thought I'd work for as long as Aisha's needed here, then maybe she and I would go for dinner?"

"Sounds great, Dad. I'm off at four."

"Do you need anything? There's Wi-Fi in the room. The password's—"

"No, no, don't tell me," Charlie interrupted her.

"The Internet's his nemesis," Aisha said dryly. "Or one of his many."

"Hey!" Charlie put a hand over his heart as if stabbed. "It's not just *my* enemy, I'll have you know. Many a writer—"

"Is a whiny, procrastinating wimp?"

"Ouch," said Jo, brown eyes twinkling—her only feature that didn't remind him of Aisha.

"So give an old whiner a kiss and get to work already."

Aisha laughed, plunked a kiss on his cheek, and left. Jo waved as she headed out of the dining room too. "Just holler if you need anything."

Charlie decided to borrow one of the still-full coffee carafes, but as he approached the island where they sat, he glanced out the window and paused. Samantha was standing in the parking lot, unaware anyone was watching her, he guessed. She stretched her arms over her head, smiled up at the sky, and appeared to take a long, deep breath. Charlie would've given anything at that minute to know what she was thinking about.

Chapter 7

THERE WAS A HINT OF heat in the bright sunlight and the energizing scent of sap filled the fresh, chilly air. Sam was surprised that she recognized the smell and even more surprised that it triggered a happy memory. Once, a long, long time ago, she had loved to take meandering walks around her Uncle Ray's property, watching for signs that the dismal winter was over and spring was actually coming.

She returned to her senses abruptly, and darted a quick glance around to make sure no one had seen her acting like a lunatic. "February is not spring in this hellhole," she muttered, yanking the tendril of hope out by its root. "It's probably not even done snowing yet."

Shortly, however, she had a bigger source of angst than the prospect of more winter. She stood on Silver's porch, repacked suitcases beside her, facing a cross-roads of sorts.

After her big bold, "I'll just stay somewhere else, no problem," promise, she was stuck. Every single place in town, even a couple nasty little dives she didn't think she could actually bring herself to stay at, was booked solid because of some stupid sports tournament. Leave it to Crotch-itch, oh, sorry, *Greenridge*, to not have enough hotels to support its events. Good news for Jo and Callum's business though.

Her gut said this was a sign, that she should snag Aisha for a couple hours this afternoon, take her shopping for anything she needed, exchange a few words and hit the road. But remembering Aisha's expression, when she'd first suggested that she might leave early, stopped her.

Jo had said the girl didn't have any expectations, but Jo was obviously overly optimistic and slightly delusional, as usual. Aisha's face looked just like Jo's, and it was just as readable. She absolutely had expectations and hopes of Sam. In fact, maybe that was the real reason, lack of a place to stay or not, Sam's whole mind and body were on the same page: flee.

Still . . . she had a plan. She was supposed to hang out here until she figured out what she was tackling next. And while it used to be lovely to flit from one city to the next, country-to-country—she couldn't believe she was thinking this—now the prospect felt a little old. Maybe the "new" thing she should try for a while was staying put. Not in Brain-glitch, of course, but somewhere.

So the question was what to do. . . . If she told Jo what was up, Jo would go into fix-it mode and drive her nuts until she found a solution—one that would no doubt be hideous, like suggesting she "bunk down" (that was a Jo phrase all right!) with her and Callum or something equally awful. Barf. The last thing she needed was to have her nose rubbed in how happy her ex-lawyer—the traitor!—and her little sister had ended up. Pleased for them or not, it was still completely nauseating.

Yet if Sam turned that idea down, Jo might call and cancel her clients, which would be stupid, kindly intentioned or not. Or she wouldn't turn them down, Sam would depart, and Jo would waste time feeling badly and/or Aisha would feel bad, too—and Sam would feel even more like a bitch than she usually did.

No, there was only one viable option that stood out as perfectly clear. If it was still on the table, that is. Damn, damn, triple damn—if only it had been her suggestion in the first place, then taking him up on it wouldn't make him the hero. Ah, well. It couldn't be helped.

Sam left her suitcases and made her way carefully down the walkway and around the cedar trees, keeping her weight on the balls of her shoes in the hopes of sparing her heels too much damage from the sharp stones.

A snuffling-grunt came from the hedge in front of Rainbow cabin. She froze. Were there bears around here? Good grief. That's exactly how she did not want to die: eaten by some mangy bear.

"Hello?" she called.

No answer. Of course. Just what she needed on top of everything else. To go insane.

She took the three stairs to Rainbow cabin's porch. A wind chime of copper wire and bright bits of colored glass and antique spoons caught her eye. It was much prettier than you'd think something made of junk would be, and though it tinkled and sang in her wake, no one stirred inside the small house.

She walked the length of the porch and caught a glimpse of Charles sitting on the couch, laptop resting on his legs, typing feverishly. Mad at herself for the unintentional Peeping Tom behavior, Sam zipped back to the door. Yet quick as her glimpse had been, she'd have to be blind to miss the intense focus and pleasure on his face. How long had it been since she'd enjoyed the satisfaction and absorption that came with a project you believed in? She stamped her foot. Great—now she was not only slightly attracted to Charles, she was jealous of him too?

No, you're neither of those things, she reprimanded herself. Not even close. You don't find him attractive because he's not your type, plus he's self-righteous and annoying. And what's to envy? Some Mr. Mom who writes drivel and puts his life on hold to follow his pregnant daughter on her freaky hormone-driven journey around the province? The guy probably had more estrogen than she did. She thought of Charlie's chest and arms and recanted the last thought, but didn't feel any less incensed. Why the heck was she tiptoeing about? This had been his brilliant idea in the first place.

She rapped on the door before she could change her mind.

Chapter 8

Gil stood and stretched, then padded barefoot to the kitchen. He considered putting on a shirt, but hanging out in your boxers all day was about the only perk of permanent bachelorhood. And despite his incredibly stupid decision last night in regards to Simone, that's what he was: a committed bachelor.

He'd done the relationship thing and what had it ever brought him besides pain and more pain? Whoever first penned the line, "Tis better to have loved and lost than to have never loved at all" was a blooming idiot. Even now the thought of Gina made him want to simultaneously weep and blow something up. The kind of love they'd shared was a once in a lifetime gift, the kind of thing that couldn't be repeated. It didn't matter if he was lonely as hell sometimes. He'd had the best once and could never—would never—settle for less.

"UGH," CHARLES MUTTERED. HE CHECKED his word count, sighed, and continued on. He'd find his groove eventually. He just had to persevere. The story, whatever it actually was, would reveal itself soon. He just had to keep putting crumbs of words out until there was a path he could follow.

> Gil opened the fridge, grabbed a beer and popped the top—so wait, make that two perks: drinking beer with breakfast was also pretty great. He settled back on the couch and against his will, despite all his newly thought thoughts—

"'Newly thought thoughts?' Are you kidding me?" It was all Charlie could do to not throw his laptop against the wall in disgust.

> Simone walked into Gil's mind in all her glory, those sad, haunting eyes of hers at war with her slightly mocking smile.
> "It was a moment of weakness," he muttered aloud, but before he could finish the thought there was a knock at the door. Expecting a parcel from Cymax, he got up.
> It wasn't the delivery guy. It was Simone. And fully dressed or not—his body remembered her. Even worse. So did his heart. How brutal—but how wonderful—those brief moments of forgetting had been. Of laughing and talking. Of not being alone.

A sharp rap on the door made Charlie jump—talk about the power of imagination—no, wait, there really was someone knocking. Shoot, for the first time since he'd started working that afternoon, he actually wanted to know what was going to happen next.

He walked across the living room, opened the door, expecting Aisha, thinking maybe she was done early.

His mouth fell open and he could only gawk. Samantha stood at his threshold, unfit for the elements as usual, in a light-knit jersey dress. From the looks of it, the weather was nippy—

Stop it, he commanded himself and met her eyes. "Ah, Sam. Hey. What's up?"

She raised an eyebrow and grinned, and he noticed she really did have a lovely mouth—oh, shit. Shit! How could he not have realized it until now? He'd based Gil's Simone on Samantha. He had to change that. Like immediately. He just had to get her to leave first. Not that anyone here likely read his books or would ever put two and two together, but it was too humiliating—even in his own mind.

"Soooo," she said. "This is kind of awkward, but I was wondering . . . were you serious when you said I could stay with you for a bit?"

Charlie's heart pounded. He did a quick scan of the porch behind Sam, but it was empty. She was alone. Was this some kind of game she was playing? Why the change of mind all of a sudden? She'd been right on all counts back in the dining room: the set up was already a little too cozy.

A shadow crossed her eyes, darkening her sea green irises to gray, but her smile remained in place.

She shifted her weight foot to foot—another pair of heels again, a lush deep purple this time. He wanted to write them off as ridiculous, but couldn't quite. They were, even if he'd only admit it to himself, smashing on her.

For some reason he couldn't articulate he found himself worried. Really worried. He shook his head.

"Okay," she said. "I understand. I get it." She turned toward the steps.

"No, no, you don't. I was just, never mind. It's fine, of course. I offered and I meant it."

Samantha's eyes fixed on his and seemed to see much deeper into him than he was comfortable with. "Okay then," she said. "Thanks, and don't worry. I won't stay long."

He held back a sigh. That she'd stay on was exactly what he was afraid of—but also, he realized, exactly what he hoped. It would be nice if he could get on the same page with his own thoughts.

He held up a finger—not *the* finger, for the record, not like she'd given him before they'd met—to say he'd be just a second. Inside, he slipped on shoes, rolled his neck side to side and cracked his knuckles, then headed back to her.

"I'll get your things," he said.

"Just like that?"

"Yep."

"Great. They're on the porch waiting for you. I'll go tell Jo the happy news that I'm slumming for a while."

Despite himself, Charles laughed. Whatever you might think about Samantha Kendall, you couldn't say she didn't speak her mind.

Sam was nowhere to be seen when Charles returned to the cabin, backbreaking suitcases in tow. He hefted them to the room opposite his, then strode to the tiny bathroom, conscious they'd be sharing it. He wasn't one to notice bathrooms except for when he was writing about them, but given her enthusiasm the other night, he couldn't help but try to see it through her eyes. Was cozy actually cramped? And how about the small round window at the foot of the tub with a great view of the mountains? Would she think it was super cool like he did, or just weird? Oh well, beggars couldn't be choosers. She'd have to deal—and that thought made him shake his head. If staying in this undeniably nice cabin was something to deal with, Samantha needed a reality check.

He peered around once more, then gathered his toiletries and stashed them in his room. He hadn't shared a washroom with a woman since Maureen—and before that only with his roommates at school—but he knew the drill. Sam didn't strike him as the low maintenance type. This way, she could take over the counter and drawers as needed.

He fetched his laptop and the box of pictures and clippings that inspired his muse, about to take it to the small desk in his bedroom. Working at a desk wasn't

his favorite thing—he preferred more casual seating—
but at least he'd have privacy.

There was a soft knock even though he'd left the
bedroom door wide open.

"You don't have to knock," he said.

She shrugged and stepped in. "Just feels a bit
weird. I'm totally invading your space. I'm sorry."

It was his turn to shrug.

"What are you doing?" she asked.

"Moving my work stuff."

She looked horrified. "You don't have to do that on
my account."

"It's no problem. And I don't work well with other
people around."

"I won't hang out here while you're working, or
I'll be in my room—and I won't stay long, I promise."

Won't stay long. She kept saying it, like he'd forget. He hoped she wouldn't yammer on similarly in
front of Aisha. It would be nice if Aisha didn't feel she
was just an item on an annoying list of to-dos.

"Let me show you around the place," he said stiffly.

She didn't remove her shoes, but followed him
gamely enough.

"Kitchen, combined dining room, living room." He
moved down the five-foot hallway, pointing left then
right. "Your bedroom, my bedroom." He opened the
cedar door at the end of the hall between the two
bedrooms. "Shared bath."

She stepped inside, pivoted in a half circle, taking in every detail, then moved to the tub and bent to peer out the oddly placed window. He thought he saw her smile, but when she straightened up her face was expressionless. He'd followed her in and was now extremely aware of how close they stood to each other—and how great she smelled.

The bathroom in Silver had tons of room; you could've set up a jazz quartet with a full brass ensemble to croon to you while you soaked in there. It hadn't felt that weird to check it out with her—okay, maybe it did, just a little. Why was he so bloody conscious of her anyway? But this room? To describe the space as intimate would be an understatement.

She held his gaze and again, as was becoming all too common, he felt she saw everything inside him, including his humiliating against-his-will attraction to her, while he, also as usual, could read nothing in her eyes—which was unsettling because they were the exact same shade and shape as his daughter's. They should have seemed familiar, yet they didn't. Aisha, no matter how cool she tried to play things, was an open book, with every emotion and thought visible in her eyes to anyone who knew her even remotely. Sam's eyes? Incredibly beautiful, yes—but also incredibly guarded.

Still waters run deep, the old expression, one of Maureen's favorites, popped into his head and described Sam very well, he thought. He wondered if anyone really knew her.

She placed a hand lightly on his chest as if to casually push him out of her way—then dropped it almost immediately and stepped back, looking startled. His heart raced. "I should unpack. Thanks again for putting me up. Jo appreciates it—I mean, I appreciate it."

She moved past him and the air between them seemed to carry the weight of her, pressing against him like a physical touch.

"It's fine. You're no bother," Charlie said stiffly, much too late.

From her room he thought he heard her snicker, then whisper, "Gee, *thanks.*"

Chapter 9

SAM UNPACKED, AS SHE ALWAYS did regardless of how long she was staying, filling the dresser's drawers with folded items, then arranging a few personal knick-knacks, three framed photos, and her perfume collection on its smooth shiny surface. She took more time than needed to hang her clothes and carefully store her shoes and boots in the closet, hoping with every stretching minute that Charles would leave, but oh, no—he kept puttering around. First he made tea, or put the kettle on anyway because she heard the telltale shriek. Then she heard the rumble of the TV. Wasn't he supposed to be visiting his kid? Then the hypocrisy hit her. Wasn't *she*?

This was not going to work. It just wasn't.

She slid her journal and pen into the corner-fitting desk's drawer, and set up her laptop and external hard drive.

She could still hear him. What was he doing now? It sounded like he was exercising of all things. She sat on the edge of the bed, scrubbed her face with her fists, and wished her senses weren't still tingling with memories of his scent. In the tiny washroom, standing so, so close, bodies nearly touching, it had been all she could do not to run her fingers through his hair. She'd almost given in—the urge to tuck it off his face so she could see his eyes practically overpowering. Thank God something deep inside overrode her insanity. Still, his face had told her all too well that he'd sensed the weird, needy vibe coming off her, too. He must think she was a freak! But she wasn't usually like this. She wasn't.

Finally, she came to her senses. If he wasn't going to leave the cabin, she was—but first she was going to clear the air, set up some roommate details, and stop acting like an idiot.

He *was* exercising. Doing hammer curls, to be specific, with twenty-five pound weights. He stopped abruptly when she entered the room and his face turned bright red. He lowered the weights, then pushed them between the couch and the wall so they were hidden from sight.

She cocked her head and studied his biceps, then caught what she was doing. Her cheeks warmed as she realized she was literally about to lick her lips. What was she? A parody of desire and desperateness? Maybe her new life plan should include a little rest time in a sanitarium for a while. Still, he did have nice arms—

She nipped that thought in the bud. "I'll call some

hotels again and ask them to put me on a cancellation list, so I get a room as soon as one's available."

"You don't have to do that."

I do so, she thought.

"In the meantime, though . . . I'm heading to town to pick up some groceries, so I'm not imposing on Jo all the time. Is there anything you'd like?"

"You have to forgive me," Charles said like she hadn't spoken. "I'm not used to living with anyone except Aisha these days—and I'm not really fit for normal company, let alone beautiful company. It makes me act . . . awkwardly or something."

Beautiful company? Sam was used to all sorts of flattery and come-ons and considered herself jaded and immune, but somehow Charlie's simple, silly words flustered her. "Well, I am beautiful, so you should find me beautiful—but you don't need to be awkward. We had a kid together. Can't be more familiar than that, right?"

She meant the comment as a joke, an icebreaker to help find common ground. And they *were* both here for Aisha—but the minute the words escaped, a storm clouded Charlie's face making it obvious she'd said the absolute wrong thing yet again.

"*We* don't have anything together," he said. "And I don't need your help. Aisha and I are shopping this afternoon for some things she needs, too. I'll grab what I want then."

Sam lifted her chin. "Suit yourself. Sorry I asked."

Bastard. For every one step they took forward, they took three back. Whenever she started to think he might not be a complete ass, that maybe she hadn't been a lunatic to choose him and Maureen for Aisha, he acted the way he was acting now, like an arrogant cold fish, and put her off completely—which was saying something because she could be a snobby, cold-fish bitch herself. And that reminded her. . . .

She widened her eyes in overt, obviously faked concern. "Oh, shoot. You were planning to take Aisha shopping *today*? That's funny, we just arranged a girls' afternoon, and she mentioned a few things she wanted a woman's advice on that I said I'd buy for her. We're getting together when she's done work."

Charles stuttered. "What? How? No, I'm meeting her after work—at four."

Sam held her hands out, palms up, and shrugged lightly. There had been a conversation sort of like that, after all. Maybe she'd left out a detail or two, like how Aisha had responded to her offer with a stiff, "Thank you, but I work till three-thirty, then I'm hanging out with my dad," and they'd set aside time for the following day instead—but close enough.

Charles looked like someone had punched him in the face, and Sam would've felt bad except she'd learned long ago that it was always better to be the puncher than the one who got punched. He'd find out she had lied soon enough, but it wouldn't matter. Hopefully by then she'd have a new place to stay. And if she didn't, well, it would have to be good-bye River's Sigh. Aisha would just have to be content with a coffee and a so long, see ya, been nice to meet ya.

Chapter 10

CHARLES CROSSED THE GRAVEL IN long strides, barely noticing the deep chill, his anger keeping him warm. How could Aisha do that to him? It wasn't like her to randomly ditch someone or break her word—but then again, she'd never had her birth mom in the picture before. And she was about to become a mom herself, something she fully admitted terrified her. His pace slowed. His fury waned. After all, it wasn't Aisha he was angry at. It was the situation. The boy that had been man enough to impregnate his daughter, but wouldn't man up and be a father. The extended family that seemed able to offer Aisha everything he and she both longed for, that he couldn't provide. Sam who flirted and snarked practically simultaneously, apparently with absolutely no awareness of the effect she had on him—and the power she had to hurt his daughter. *Their* daughter, the "kid they had together." And what the hell was that crack supposed to mean anyway? Was she already reneging on her plans to move on and leave them be?

He opened the door to the lodge's communal din-ing/meeting room too hard. It slammed against the wall.

Aisha glanced over, then suddenly pressed her hand against her ample side.

"Are you all right?" he asked panicked, all thoughts of Samantha Kendall momentarily forgotten, just as Aisha said at the same time, "Dad, what the hell?"

"Sorry," he muttered. "I didn't know it would fly back into the wall like that."

"I'm fine," she replied.

But he didn't like the flush in her cheeks or the dampness of the curls that had escaped her messy bun and framed her face. "You look like you're in pain."

"And you look like you're going to freeze to death. I thought we were going up town. Why aren't you wearing a coat?"

"You're not wearing a coat either."

"Dad!" Her tone was both exasperated and amused. "I weigh ten tons. I feel like I'll never be remotely cool, in any sense of the word, ever again."

He laughed and then her full statement hit him. "Wait, *we*—as in you and I—are still going up town when you get off today?"

One of Aisha's dramatically arched brows that she was so proud of—and so careful to maintain—rose. "Are you on crack? We just made the plan last night."

"Yeah, but—" It was on the tip of his tongue to say

Sam had told him there'd been a change. Why would she say that if it wasn't true? Was it an honest mistake? If so, should he postpone with Aisha? A memory of Sam's raised chin just before her wide-eyed "sadness" about the misunderstanding and implied cancellation flashed into his head.

A small grunt of realization escaped him. What a—

Before he finished that thought his own words came back to him. He had been kind of a jerk to her simple question about whether he wanted her to pick something up for him. Still, lying about who had plans with Aisha? What was she, twelve?

Aisha's voice broke through the whirl of contradictory thoughts scudding through his head. "What is up with you? Are you okay?"

"I'm fine, just thought I'd gotten my wires crossed or something. Sorry."

"Whatever." Aisha flapped her hand dismissively, but her expression said she wasn't convinced he was "fine" in the slightest. "I've just gotta pee, *again*, and we can go."

"Sure, babe. Sounds good."

She disappeared and he paced the room, then positioned himself near one of the windows. Every view from anywhere in the whole frigging River's Sigh enterprise was postcard worthy. It was totally depressing.

A door clicked open behind him and he turned, expecting to see Aisha—but his gaze rested on Sam instead.

She flinched a little, then something in her face hardened and she glided toward him in that walk of hers that he—much to his despair—appreciated all too much.

"Charles," she said formally.

"Samantha," he said, matching her tone, but speaking softly. He wanted to call her on her juvenile lie, but also didn't want to tip his hand and show he was onto her. What game would she play next?

Her mouth—some shade of deep plum today—tightened for a second, then her milk-white teeth worried the corner of her plump bottom lip. Something in his loins went a little crazy. And why did she have to wear that subtle perfume all the time? It was indecent.

She sighed, smiled a tad ruefully and wrinkled her nose—and when she spoke again, he knew he looked shocked. Whatever he'd been expecting her to say it wasn't what came next. "So, yeah ... about the whole Aisha afternoon thing. As you've probably already deduced, I lied. I did ask her if we could meet today, maybe go shopping. . . . I thought it might be less uncomfortable then staring at each other for an hour in a restaurant or something. Less pressure, you know?"

Charlie found he couldn't speak. He nodded.

"But she told me flat out it wouldn't work. That she was meeting you. So yeah," she repeated. "I'm sorry."

He studied her face, unsure of what exactly he was looking for in her perfectly made-up features and glass-smooth expression. "I'm glad you told me. I was going to read her the riot act for standing me up without any notice."

Sam returned his look, and to him it seemed like all they'd done since they'd met was try to stare each other down. Then her mouth, that delicious mouth, quirked and smile lines crinkled by her eyes. He liked the tiny wrinkles a lot, how they softened her face, gave her away just a little. He wanted to reach out and trace them with one finger. He shoved his hands in his pockets.

"You already knew, didn't you?" she asked.

Truth or lie. "Yeah," he admitted.

"Before or after you read her the 'riot act'?"

"Before."

The fledgling smile faded and she nodded. "So now she knows I'm a big liar." It wasn't a question.

He wanted to nod. It would serve her right—and it was what she deserved . . . or maybe not. What a person "deserved" was a dangerous thing to start tossing judgment around about.

"Are you—a liar, I mean?" he asked instead, surprising himself—and her too, from the startled expression that flitted across her face. She recovered quickly, was carefully blank and smooth again.

"Sometimes."

Footsteps and the jingle of Aisha's handbag kept

him from replying. "I'm ready," Aisha's voice piped from the hall, quickly followed by her reappearance in the room and a much quieter, "Oh . . . hi. Sorry, I didn't know you were here."

"Yeah, but I was just leaving. Have fun." Samantha gave Charles a little wave. "I'll see you later."

Aisha nodded, but her gaze swung from Sam to Charlie and she shot him a look that he couldn't read—a perfect fit with the recurring theme of his life these days: Charles Bailey is completely unable to make sense of or understand his life or the people in it.

As he followed his rotund daughter out to the car, his mind rested on Samantha again. What kind of a liar admits she's a liar? A pathological one or a "liar" that really isn't a liar at all? In any case, the woman was obviously messed up—maybe even as messed up as he was—but somehow they had to come to an understanding, so Aisha would be protected from potential hurt as much as possible. And he, as much as he dreaded it, better work on getting a life of his own again so he'd stop having this raging interest in the entirely inappropriate, all-wrong-for-him Samantha. After all, the only possible reason for him to have these spasms of attraction for her—someone who was his opposite in every way that mattered—was because he'd been in such a deep sleep of grief and now, whether he was ready or not, his body and brain were waking up and getting ideas. He needed to kindle new relationships and rebuild friendships. Not romantic ones, of course. He'd had one love, his true love, and he'd settle for nothing less—now where had he heard that or thought that before? It sounded familiar. No matter. Usually he had amazing self-control and discipline. He would conscientiously meet other adults, have adult conversations, make some friends. . . . He'd be able to live perfectly fine if those small comforts even partially compensated for the hole Maureen had left in him.

He shivered as he climbed into the driver's seat and slammed the door. He'd be darned if he couldn't smell snow. It wasn't really going to snow in February, was it? That would be just his luck.

Beside him Aisha went through the ordeal of securing her seatbelt around her beach ball belly, but she kept darting glances at him, and he knew it wouldn't be long before her interrogation started. But what could he say? There was nothing to say. No news to report. Just her to think about. Her and the baby.

Charles Bailey becomes a grandparent, lets extended family heal his heart, and learns that romantic love is only one type of love—and maybe not even the most important type. Yes, that would be his life's new storyline.

As he rolled out of the parking lot, he felt cautiously optimistic, despite the threat of the approaching cold spell.

Chapter 11

SAM WAS STANDING IN THE checkout line, a small grocery cart packed full. She couldn't help it. She shopped when she was stressed—and somehow even tins of soup were soothing. She fidgeted with the strap on her oversized leather bag, and sipped her deliciously fragrant Chai. Whoever initially thought of putting coffee kiosks into grocery stores was brilliant.

Her ode to beverages was interrupted up by a boisterous, testosterone-filled purr. "Sam, is that you? You're back? You look amazing."

She sighed inwardly, but readied herself for the social game. Putting a friendly smile on her face, she pivoted to face the huge blond guy greeting her with a big grin of his own. "Dave—hey. I'm flattered you remember who I am, let alone what I look like."

"Like a guy could ever forget you."

Sam wanted to roll her eyes and ask him what planet he lived on. After all, he had to live in a different world if he thought they were friends. It hadn't been that long since he'd done all he could to wreck Jo and Callum's relationship. She'd practically had to drag him by his ear to Jo's to get him to straighten out the huge rift he'd caused with his lies. For all she knew he was still pining to get into Jo's pants. He was scheming, two-faced, pathetic, transparently lonely, and really good-looking—so naturally she also identified with him and couldn't help but like him a little. Dave was in the candy bar category of men, not good for you at all and not the same quality as real chocolate—but tempting and sort of yummy all the same. The analogy made her smile more sincerely.

"So how are things, Dave?"

By the time she was through the checkout line, she'd accepted Dave's invitation to work out at his gym, but turned down his offer of a free membership. (She only joked about letting guys pay. She'd learned the hard way that nothing was free the year she got pregnant with Aisha.) She'd even said maybe to going out for dinner. Jo would think she was nuts—nothing new there—but if Sam didn't have the odd invite to leave the bed-and-breakfast, she'd go nuts for real.

He walked her out to the Mercedes and whistled softly when he got close to it—which earned him a point. She was still a little awed by her ride, too. As a kid she'd planned to have money, to be able to buy not only things she needed but also things she wanted— and yet a tiny part of her was still surprised she'd made it happen. And she didn't rest easy either. She was all too aware that the minute you relaxed, felt this was it, life was finally secure, the rug was bound to be pulled out from under you.

Dave was saying something.

"Pardon? I'm sorry, I got distracted for a second."

Dave leaned against the SUV, solidly losing the point he'd just gained. "By me, I hope."

More like you wish, Sam thought. She laughed and smiled. (Sometimes she felt like a damned marionette. Laugh, smile, twirl—and again. And again.)

"What?" Dave's tone changed, became slightly alarmed. "Did I say something wrong?"

"No, no, I'm just preoccupied with some stuff." *Like a mental breakdown.*

Dave stepped away from her, which meant he moved off the Mercedes. One good thing. "Is this 'stuff' anything I can help with?"

"No. Thanks though. You're sweet."

She opened the passenger door and placed her grocery bags in one by one. Apparently her words, tone and gesture reassured him that she wasn't going to be all needy. "I'm serious about dinner, Samantha."

She faced him, and rested her hand on his chest. He looked down and his smile grew. Yep, transparent and pathetic, all right—but all too easy to manipulate. Not kindred spirits at all then. Her empathy waned. "We'll see, Dave. We'll see."

THE EVENING PASSED UNEVENTFULLY. SAM went for a walk, wanting to get a better look at the other cabins.

She had tried the first evening—the night she'd come across Charlie staring at the door to Silver cabin—but it had been too dark.

Now she was delighted by what she saw in the other three rentals. "Chinook" was the largest. It looked big enough to house a family and had its own fenced yard, complete with a small wooden fort and jungle gym thing for kids.

"Spring" was the most hidden and out of the way. It was bizarrely tall and narrow. Perhaps there was a room per floor? It was also the most beaten up, obviously still going through the renovation process.

"Minnow" was significantly smaller than the rest, with a tiny sheltered porch that housed a large black rocking chair. An oval platform rested on the porch railing beside the chair, serving as a table. Very clever. She had to hand it to Jo. The whole property was cute as a button, but in a relaxed, artsy way—not frou-frou or fussy.

She walked along a well-beaten trail and came across two more graying cabins that had been framed and roofed, then deserted before completed. Sam didn't know if they'd be easily restored or renovated, but felt pleased nonetheless. There was definitely room for Jo and Callum to grow the business, should they wish to. A bittersweet pang of pride and happiness hit her. Jo was really doing it. Risking everything—all the money she'd inherited from their Uncle Ray's place and her heart once more to the guy who had originally crushed it—to build the home and business she'd always envisioned. She was a fool to do so, of course, but a brave, admirable one at least.

Back in Rainbow, chilled but surprisingly mellow, she changed into a pair of paisley print men's pajamas. Then she ate a can of chunky pea soup for dinner, enjoyed a bourbon and ginger ale—just one—and retired to her room to read and check out her long-term stock charts, wanting to be out of the way whenever Charlie returned.

At some point, tucked into the admittedly gorgeous and seductive Egyptian cotton sheets and down duvet, she dozed off. It was late when the click of the cabin's front door and a soft rumble of voices woke her. For a second she wondered where she was. When she remembered, she curled onto her side and tucked her pillow close. As she relaxed into the hazy comfort of dropping back to sleep, she indulged in a game she'd played as a girl the odd time she slept over at a rare friend's house—imagining that the household noises and family sounds belonged to her home, her family.

Chapter 12

A HARD CRUST OF FROZEN slush-snow covered everything, turning it all—the deck, the railing, the stairs, the whole parking lot—into a treacherous slipping risk.

"Damn. We didn't expect to need someone out to gravel and salt this late in the year," Jo fretted, then added, "And how do you even walk in those things? If you fall, it's your own fault. No suing."

Sam laughed. "Of course I wouldn't sue you. Set myself up here permanently and let you pamper my paralyzed ass for the rest of my life, yes, but not sue—and besides, what are you complaining about anyway? I'm wearing boots."

"Yeah, right," Jo scoffed, her eyes dropping to Sam's knee-high suede wedges. "*These* are boots." She lifted her left leg and waggled her foot to show off the clunky felt-packed, rubber-soled monstrosity she sported—then almost lost her balance and clutched Sam for support.

"Hey—you're the one who's going to make us both fall. And those aren't boots. They're embarrassments."

They both giggled and continued to half-mince, half-glide toward the main house.

"I just hope it stays cold. If it warms up another degree or two, we'll get a hideous dump of snow."

Sam raised her eyebrow. "I thought you 'adore' snow?"

Jo lightly punched Sam's arm. "I do. Just more so pre-Christmas and less so when I'm looking forward to spring and hoping no one falls to their deaths on my property."

A blaring series of loud beeps carried in the still morning air, warning that a heavy vehicle was backing up, followed by the roar of a heavy-duty engine crawling along the driveway.

"They managed to fit us in," Jo said. "Thank goodness."

"Yeah, a no death policy at your bed-and-slip-fest is a good idea, for sure," Sam agreed. They made their way into the dining room where not a sign of breakfast was left, though a fragrant memory of it lingered in the air.

"You missed out," Jo said. "Can I make you something?"

"No, and don't you dare offer that option to other guests either. End your breakfast promptly at nine on weekdays and eleven on weekends, as advertised, or you'll get a reputation for being easy and you'll end up cooking all day, every day."

"Well, I sure wouldn't want a reputation for being easy," Jo deadpanned. Callum chose that moment to walk in from the kitchen and gave her a very funny look, causing Jo and Sam to burst out laughing. He shook his head and retreated the way he'd come, which only made them giggle harder.

"Are you sure you're all right staying with Charlie?" Jo asked.

"Absolutely. We've come to a perfect arrangement. We don't speak and we don't see each other. Seriously, I worked in my room in the early hours, then left for most of the day and he went off for most of the night. If things stay like this, it's ideal."

Jo shook her head. "He's not a terrible guy, you know. Your instincts about him and Maureen all those years ago were right on the money. Aisha is a great person, smart, funny, strong—and I think she deeply loved her parents and grew up knowing she was deeply loved in return."

"Yeah, yeah, all's swell that ends up with a runaway, pregnant teen."

"Okay, wow. That's not fair, or even accurate. Aisha's not a runaway. And yes, she's young, but she's graduated, at least. And as for her belly full of 'Surprise!' . . . in case it's slipped your mind, that happens to the best of us, occasionally."

"Yeah, yeah," Sam repeated and helped herself to a coffee from the beverage caddy. She kept her back turned to Jo, taking her time doctoring her mug. "And what do I say to her? What do we talk about? She probably hates me or will when she gets to know me."

Jo patted Sam's shoulder and her hand was a comforting weight, but whatever words Jo might've added for extra encouragement were cut off.

The dining room door swung open. "Oh, you beat me here? Sorry. I'm ready whenever you are." Aisha sounded confident and casual, like they met and hung out all the time.

Sam massaged her temples once, then turned. "Sounds great." She was beyond relieved that her voice sounded just as chipper and calm as Aisha's had.

Their drive to downtown Greenridge was only slightly awkward. Aisha directed Sam where to turn and Sam let her, despite knowing the place well. At least they weren't dead silent. They ended up at the funky little coffee shop on Main Street called The Zoo.

Sam had no idea what kind of person dreamed up the idea to decorate a restaurant with life-sized wire sculptures of animals, but somehow it really worked— and had the added bonus of being a conversation starter. As she and Aisha waited in line for their beverages—chai tea lattes for both of them—they decided on favorites. Aisha loved them all, but was particularly enamored with two baby elephants, one sitting, one standing, behind a low couch.

"They're just so cute. I love how the one holds his sister's tail in his trunk."

Yeah, almost too cutesy. Sam voted for a giraffe

almost hidden from view by a large leafy tree in the back corner of room.

The rest of the visit was paradoxically both smoother and more bizarre than Sam had anticipated. It reminded Sam of a job interview (one she wasn't quite sure she was nailing) by someone who'd obviously done her homework and knew a lot about the person she was interviewing. Aisha had obviously drilled Jo, too.

Aisha brought up nurture versus nature, expressing surprise. She'd always believed that nurture trumped all, but now that she'd met Jo and Sam and noticed weird similarities and idiosyncrasies between herself and them—the types of things she previously would've thought you picked up from people you lived with—she felt genetics were extremely powerful. She found that both fascinating and disheartening. Sam couldn't help but relate.

Aisha asked intelligent questions about how Sam had made her money on the stock market in the past, why she wasn't a day trader anymore, and how she currently lived off her investments.

Sam tried to not feel criticized when Aisha shook her head and mused, "I couldn't do that. I want to do something that helps other people or the environment or something. I could never just be interested in money for the sake of making more money or having money."

Sam fidgeted with an empty creamer and forced a chuckle. "Well, don't knock it 'til you've ever lived without it."

Aisha gave her a look, then nodded.

They exchanged lists of likes and dislikes, including silly things like favorite pastimes and foods. Sam was relieved by the safety of this new direction, only to be shown as the end of their hour approached that Aisha had lulled her into a false sense of comfort.

"So I purposely avoided questions about my birth father and circumstances surrounding my adoption, and what your thoughts are about whether I should keep the bean"—she pointed at her belly—"or give her to someone else, but I'd like you to think about it and give me as much info and advice as you're comfortable with, soon."

Aisha might be seventeen in earth years, Sam thought, but she was eighty in alien-daughter years.

As they walked out of The Zoo, Aisha waved good-bye to the multi-pierced young guy behind the counter. Sam noticed he blushed and she raised an eyebrow at Aisha. "New flame?"

Aisha shook her head—too vigorously, if you asked Sam—and motioned at her stomach. "Nah. I'm like four hundred months pregnant."

"If you say so." Sam shrugged.

Just before Sam climbed into the Mercedes, after making sure Aisha didn't need a ride anywhere, Aisha added, "It looks like we could've talked longer, but I didn't want it to be too much, you know?"

Sam nodded.

"Same time and place tomorrow?"

"You bet. Sounds good." Sam watched Aisha move away, surprisingly light on her feet considering her bulk, and then started the vehicle.

She shared Aisha's opinion that the visit hadn't been as grueling as it could've been, but she wasn't fully reassured. After all, Aisha's "think about it" comment said it all. This had been the easy session. The hard stuff, the things Sam didn't like thinking about let alone talking about, was yet to come.

CHARLES TRIED TO WORK. HE really did. But he needed tea (lemon-ginseng to be exact). And then he needed a long hot shower. And then he figured he should tidy up because . . . well, for no good reason, actually. He was totally stalling and he totally knew why. It had grown dark. Late afternoon had stretched into evening and now it was night—and Samantha and Aisha still weren't back.

Yet he was 99.9 percent confident they were safe, were probably just getting along as well as he'd feared, had "hit it off" as the saying goes. After all, he'd texted Aisha as many times as he could get away with and she'd responded each time with little smiling emoticons or one word answers that told him nothing except she was fine.

Still when you were as pregnant as Aisha, things

could change in an instant—and she'd worried him yesterday. She seemed like she was in pain—yet she insisted all was well, that he was "as usual" being a freak and worrying about nothing. He paced while his open laptop glared at him from across the shadowy room. . . . Aisha would just have to suck it up. He wasn't a freak. He was a parent. And parents worried. That's what they did. Obsessively. Compulsively. Against their own will, for crying out loud! And if kids came with how-to-raise-them manuals (like they should!), there would've been a full chapter devoted to the subject, titled something catchy like, "Worrying About Your Child—and why you shouldn't worry that you worry because it's unavoidable."

He stared out the window once more. The day's earlier frigid temperatures had eased, which only worsened the weather. The cold gleam of the parking lot's lone streetlight revealed a punishing mixture of snow and ice-rain pellets hurtling toward the ground.

His phone beeped. In his race to answer, he almost upended the big easy chair between him and the coffee table.

A reply to his last text. He could hear Aisha's annoyance, despite her purple balloon letter font. "Turning off phone. At movie. TTYT."

Talk to you tomorrow, hey? He wished she'd at least pop by the cabin to say good-night, so he'd know when she got back safe and sound. He fired off a quick reply saying just that, hoping she'd get the message before she clicked off.

Determined to bang out a couple hundred words before he gave up altogether and climbed into his car to "casually" go find them, he sat back down on the couch.

He reread his last paragraph and was freshly reminded of how he'd based Simone on Samantha. His hands hovered over the keyboard as he tried to reimagine her, but then he shook his head. He was being stupid. No one but him cared where he drew inspiration from—and Simone was based on an imaginary version of Sam anyway. No doubt the character would change and grow and become unrecognizably different in every way. He was just looking for reasons to procrastinate. Besides . . . he couldn't believe he was even admitting this to himself, it was kind of fun to have a muse. It had been a long time and maybe that was another bonus. Readers would probably welcome a new type of heroine from him.

"Okay then, back to it," he muttered and commenced typing.

His first instinct was to slam the door, pretend he hadn't opened it to her in the first place—but then Simone smiled and Gil couldn't just slam *it.*

"Look, Simone. You seem great—I mean you are great."

The smile fell from her face, and she shoved her hands into her pockets. "I see," she said.

"It's just—"

"No, don't worry. I get it."

She did? Well, that was amazing because Gil sure as hell didn't. Before he could process that thought— and the scalding emotions that poured through him and felt all too much like regret, she turned and left.

Gil forgot he was holding a beer in his hurry to close and deadbolt the door behind Simone. Amber liquid sloshed over the top and spilled onto the floor. He stared at the mess for a long time. He could clean it up, do his best to remove all traces, but that wouldn't change what had happened. The mess was made. It was out of the can. There was no going back. There was a parallel message in those thoughts that he wanted to ignore.

Charlie stretched and resumed his hunched position. A minute later he jumped as a key turned in the lock.

Samantha tiptoed in, a notable contrast to her usual purposeful stride or cocky swagger. She started when she saw him. "Oh . . . hi. Sorry. All the lights are out. I thought you were in bed."

"I was waiting up," Charlie said, clicking on a lamp, all too aware of how he sounded—like he was a grouchy overbearing father. Which he was. But still, who wanted to sound like one?

She nodded and moved toward her room, sodden boots clenched in her right hand. Her hair and jacket were dripping.

"What on earth were you guys doing? Aisha's ready to go into labor any day. I hope you didn't wear her out."

Samantha turned, eyes narrowed. "You're worried I kept your adult-lives-on-her-own daughter up past her bedtime?"

"She's not quite an adult, and it's not the hour that concerns me. It's her condition—and that it's hideous out there."

"She lives on her own, seems to be planning to from here on out. And her 'condition' is motherhood. Sounds pretty adult to me."

Charlie winced. He and Aisha had had this conversation too, many times, but he was still trying to talk her out of it. Seventeen was pretty young to be completely self-sufficient, though if anyone could do it and thrive, it would be her.

"So where is she now?"

"No idea. I asked if she needed a ride anywhere. She said no. I haven't seen her for hours."

Oh . . . so they hadn't been visiting for ten hours. That did make more sense, but now he had a new thing to worry about. "So how's she getting home?"

"How would I know?"

"You didn't ask?"

"What? I—well, no. Were you always this controlling when she was younger?"

"It's not controlling. It's *considerate*. And things

happen—bad things. If you can stave them off with a bit of attention to detail, a bit of courtesy, why not try?"

Sam's brow furrowed and one of her eyebrows rose. "Oh, yeah, you're a genius for 'staving off things' with your attention to detail and gobs of consideration."

"What the hell is that supposed to mean?"

She ignored him. "When I last saw her, around four-thirty, she was fine. Had dinner plans with someone who helped do the renovations here. Mentioned something about a show. Said she'll text if she goes into labor and to remind you to keep your phone charged. Apparently you have a problem remembering technology requires power?"

Charlie nodded, relieved on one hand—everything sounded like Aisha to a T—and ashamed on the other. Why was he always such a grouch to Samantha? It wasn't her fault she was in their lives. In fact, she was the whole reason he even had Aisha. Maybe he should try being grateful instead of acting like an asshole. Maureen would be furious if she saw how he treated their baby's birth mom.

"So can I go now, officer, or do you have any other questions?"

Ouch—but he guessed he deserved that. He scrubbed a hand over his face. "Yeah, I do. More than a few actually."

"What? Are you kidding me?"

In the mist rising off her damp hair and clothing because of the contrast between the outdoor temperature and the heat of the cabin, he could smell traces of her shampoo mingled with the sexy perfume she always wore.

"One," he said. "Where on earth were you and what the heck were you doing to get soaked like that?"

Samantha's eyebrows shot up, and she stuck her hands on her hips.

"Two. I bet you haven't eaten a thing since lunch."

"That's a statement, not a question."

"Semantics, but point taken. Three and four: do you need me to fetch anything from the Mercedes, and would you like me to make us something to eat? I didn't have dinner. I'm starving."

The tiniest curve of a smile tugged at Samantha's mouth. "Do I need you to 'fetch' anything? Uh, no—but thank you. And as for feeding me . . . that'd be pretty great, actually. If you really don't mind."

Charlie made a shooing motion. "So go. Get cleaned up and change your clothes. You're a mess, you'll give yourself pneumonia, you're dripping on the floor—go, go, go."

Samantha looked incredulous, then burst out laughing. "Okay, okay, I get it. You're apologizing for being a control freak by being extra controlling."

He shrugged. "I have no idea what you mean."

She was at the door to her room, when she paused and turned to look back at him. "Am I allowed to ask how long I have?"

Charlie gave an exaggerated exhale of frustration. "How long do you need?"

"Half an hour?"

"*Fine.*"

She smirked again, and disappeared into her room. Moments later she was in the bathroom and he heard water running in the tub. He tried not to think of her undressing and sinking into its steamy warmth. Good grief, what was his glitch? Was he developing a bathtub fetish? He shook his head, left the lamp on, but lit some candles too, then moved to the kitchen.

Dinner was almost ready when Samantha exited the washroom. He looked up from the romaine lettuce he was tearing and glimpsed her long bare legs under what looked like some big guy's pajama top as she traipsed to her room—and he wondered why the obvious hadn't occurred to him. Of course she had some man in her life. Look at her.

He dumped a liberal amount of freshly grated Parmesan, followed by heated cream and butter, into the cooked pasta, then put the pot's lid on tightly and shook it hard to mix it.

When Sam finally appeared beside him in the kitchen, she was fully dressed in a soft-looking sweater, skinny jeans, and—surprise of surprises—ankle socks instead of her usual killer heels. The little cotton socks were just as appealing in their own way as her stilettos, he thought—then gave himself a kick. He paid way too much attention to what she wore. His focus moved to her flushed cheeks and damp hair that was pinned up in a loose twist. She made a surprised sound when she saw the table. "Why Charles Brown—wait, wait, your name is *Charlie Brown*?" She laughed hard. "How could I have missed that?"

He shook his head and emptied the pasta into a serving dish. "Because it's not. I'm Charles—a.k.a. Charlie—Bailey. Maureen was Brown. When we hyphenated Aisha's last name, we thought Bailey-Brown sounded better."

"Aisha Bailey-Brown. Aisha Brown-Bailey. You're right. Too bad though. I'd love it if your name was Charlie Brown."

He studied her. She really was pretty—especially when she was laughing.

"Of course, you're more like Lucy than Chuck," she added, grinning.

"Thanks, thanks a lot."

She didn't seem to hear him as she surveyed the table again. "I thought we'd have canned soup or something. This looks . . . great."

There was an off note in her voice. Charlie studied the fare. Fettuccine Alfredo, sauce from scratch, with plump sautéed shrimp. A big Caesar salad. Maybe she didn't like garlic? Or had a seafood allergy? Or was it the red-checked tablecloth? He'd found it in a drawer and thought it was cute, but maybe it was too much, too corny or something. Or worse, maybe it seemed like he was trying too hard to make them something they weren't, like friends or something.

She touched his arm. "It looks and smells amazing."

"But?"

She looked pained, and shook her head like she was working out some inner dilemma. "But nothing," she said finally. "Load me up."

He smiled and obeyed, but didn't relax fully until she sat down, lay napkin across her lap, and took her first mouthful. Her eyes widened. "Mmm, this is good."

"Thanks," he said, his heart skipping a little. Why did it matter so darn much whether she liked it or not?

"Wait!" She hopped up, rummaged in the fridge, then in a cupboard, and returned with a bottle of wine and two stemmed glasses.

"Is Chardonnay all right?"

"Perfect. A delicately nuanced wine for a simple, rich dish."

"Well, la-di-dah," she said, and he laughed.

He wished he'd thought of buying wine, but it hadn't even occurred to him. After all, how long had it been since he'd had wine with dinner? Too long.

She snugged herself back into the tiny table, and they were both so long legged that their knees almost touched. Charles could've happily sat there, brushed up against her, watching her enjoy her food forever. The thought made his fists clench.

As the meal progressed and the wine disappeared—only to be magically replaced by a new bottle—they relaxed and their tongues loosened. They devoured their food and drinks, exchanged trivialities and laughed a lot. It was all pretty damn great.

Samantha smiled as if she'd heard his thought and shared his contentment. "So earlier, before dinner"—she waved her hand to take in the emptied plates—"and before your invite-slash-command to join you, you were pretty funny. And fair. I'm sorry I called you controlling."

He shook his head. "No apology needed. I can be overbearing, especially when I'm worried. I know it. I'm in over my head with Aisha. I don't know what to tell her. Part of me is going mental because she hasn't made a decision about adoption or no adoption. Part of me completely gets why she hasn't. I feel responsible that she's in this predicament—and then there's you."

"Me?" Sam pointed at herself with her thumb. "What'd I do?"

"It's not what you did. It's just—never mind."

"No, what? Tell me. I'm curious." Samantha leaned back in a pleasure-filled stretch. It was all Charlie could do to keep his eyes in his head and not moan aloud. Man, the woman could wear a sweater.

He took a big mouthful of pasta to stall, taking his time chewing and swallowing. "It's nothing. Let's not talk about my messed up head. Let's talk about us."

Her pretty eyebrows rose again.

"Er—not quite what I meant."

"Too bad," she said.

He knew she was just teasing him back, but that fact didn't keep his heart from racing or knock away the idiot grin blooming across his face.

"Tell me about you," he said. "You of now, of today, not the woman who gave me and Maureen the greatest gift of our lives all those years ago."

Samantha's eyes glistened and she gave a solitary nod, acknowledging his comment. Her perfect white teeth sank into her bottom lip for just a moment. "Me now, hey? Hmm, not so different now than I was then."

"No?"

"No and anyway, I'm boring. Tell me about you."

There was no way Samantha Kendall was boring. Everything about her was fascinating, although he couldn't pinpoint exactly why he thought so. Was it his overwhelming attraction to her, or was it that in some ways he saw her as the enemy—the person who could steal the last of his family away from him—and he felt compelled to study her, to get to know her in some sort of twisted reconnaissance mission?

He shook his head. The lavish dinner was a comforting weight in his stomach and his brain was dancing with wine. For once he didn't want to overthink everything. He just wanted to feel. And just like that he knew the answer to what was so disturbing about Sam. She made him *feel* again, the whole gamut of emotion from anger to happiness to lust and frustration. . . .

Just enjoy the night, he commanded himself. You can make sense of it all later. He realized she was staring at him and knew he'd been quiet for too long.

"There's no way Samantha Kendall's boring," he repeated then grimaced at his use of the third person aloud, to her face. "Er, I mean, no way you're boring."

"Heh, yeah . . . there's nothing like a bottle of wine or two to make me scintillating."

"Great word," he said.

She laughed. "High praise from a famous author."

"Not famous. Not by a long shot. I'm a bread and butter writer at most."

"Bread and butter—cute way to put it. And it means, yes, you make your living writing books, right?"

Or that I used to, at least, he thought, but didn't correct her, just nodded.

"So what do you write? What genre?"

Genre! She must be a reader. "Romance."

She leaned in over the table. "For real?"

He nodded again. Was it a good for real or a bad for real? Not that he cared. He was just curious.

She practically squealed, which made him laugh. "What a coincidence. I read anything, but I *adore* romance." She pressed a finger to her lips and gave an exaggerated shhhh. "Don't tell anyone though, or I'll have to kill you."

"Why's it such a huge secret?"

"Come on." She looked incredulous. "I'm a big bitch. Bitches don't read romance. They're for sweet, nice little housewives. If it gets out, my rep will be ruined."

"Oh, yeah?"

"Yeah." She was still leaned in close.

Charles bent in too, like he was going in for a kiss—and God, he wanted to. He really wanted to. "I have the insider secret on that. You want to know the dirt?"

"Yes," she said eagerly, like he was actually going to say something mind-blowing.

"Devout romance readers are more varied—and more plentiful—than you think. There's no one type. And why would there be? What do any of us care about more than our relationships? What motivates us greater than love and sex? It's biology, baby."

Sam shook her head, grinning. "I guess . . . yes, you have a point."

"But?"

"Well, I admit I was expecting the 'dirt' to be a little more tawdry."

Charles laughed, then stopped abruptly.

"What?" Sam asked.

"It's just, ah, nothing."

"Stop doing that. Stop starting stuff, then buttoning up and saying it was nothing."

"Okay . . ." He poured the remaining bit of wine

into their glasses, just enough for another swallow or two each. "I was going to say that I haven't laughed so much in a long, long time. Years, actually." He forced himself to hold her gaze, and found himself surprised—then moved—by the softness in her jade eyes.

"I had fun too." She looked away. "But it's getting late and I'm tired and my whole body is screaming to stretch out and sleep—and the dishes aren't going to wash themselves."

Several excuses are always less convincing than one. The Aldous Huxley quote came to Charlie out of nowhere and struck him with mingled awe and flattered pride. Sam had quite possibly enjoyed the evening as much as he had—and might even feel similarly confused and undone by it.

Her feet, still so close to his, shifted under the table, and he sensed she was about to stand up. But he didn't want the evening to end. Tomorrow would come soon enough. Couldn't they visit and chat a little longer? Surprising himself—and her—he reached down and caught her foot, then lifted it to his lap.

"The last thing you have to worry about is the dishes. I invited you to dinner. They're on me—but before you go to bed, I have just one more question."

He kneaded her foot softly.

"Sheesh, you. Always with the questions," she whispered.

"Hey, if it's too late, it can wait, no worries." He pressed deeper into her sole and she sighed softly.

"If you keep doing that, I think I can muster up some energy to keep talking."

"I was thinking about those ridiculous shoes you always wear"—her leg tightened under his grip—"that I love, that any guy who wasn't dead would love, actually . . . " She laughed and her muscles eased. "Don't they hurt?"

"Not at all. They're good quality shoes, which makes a huge difference, and I'm pretty light on my feet—plus I've worn heels since I was eleven. I know how to walk in them."

He agreed with her last line completely, but couldn't think of a way to say it that wouldn't sound weird or creepy. *I'll say you do, hyuk, hyuk*—

"But I'm not going to lie, whether my shoes kill me or not, that feels delicious. More than delicious."

He was working her instep with both thumbs now and she was practically purring. A shudder of arousal quaked through him at her obvious pleasure. He was trying to think of something erotic—or at least not idiotic—to say in return, when a light knock at the door shut him down.

Before he or Sam could move or even say, "Come in," the door burst open and Aisha bounced into the room.

"Hey, pops. Hey, Sam. Smells fantastic in here, did—" The happy greeting died on Aisha's lips as she took in the dinner table—and Sam's foot resting in Charlie's lap.

"Well, well." Aisha glared at Charlie. "How *cozy*. When you said you were 'making out okay,' Dad, I had no idea—and you." She pinned Sam next. "I'm so glad the living arrangements are, as you said, um, 'bearable.' You guys have what, known each other two days?" A look of horror crossed her face. "Oh, sick— you knew each other when I was born too. You didn't, you wouldn't have—*gross*."

Charlie dropped Sam's foot. Sam whipped her legs under her chair and shifted as far from him as she could without physically shoving herself from the table.

"It's not what it looks like." Charlie stood and moved nearer to Aisha. She stepped back.

"It's really not." Sam got up too, but inched the opposite direction, toward the hallway.

"Oh, it's not? So you guys didn't have dinner with two bottles of wine and a follow up game of footsies?"

Put like that it did sound . . . not as nice as it actually had been. Charlie shot a look at Sam; she gave him a sad smile and a half-shrug.

Aisha fired again. "Just tell me you didn't flirt or find each other attractive when you and Mom were in the process of having me."

"You're over reacting, Aisha."

"Save it till tomorrow. I'm wiped."

"I'll walk you to your cabin."

"No, no. You obviously have your hands full."

Samantha spoke up. She was by her bedroom door

now, ready to dart out of sight. "Listen to him—and let him walk you. It's icy out."

Aisha glanced her direction, but Sam was gone, the door clicking shut behind her.

Charles walked Aisha back to Minnow and reiterated that while he could see how Aisha thought it looked "cozy," it really was innocent. They'd had a nice dinner, yes. They'd chatted, yes. He was massaging her foot—big deal. They were both just interested in Aisha's wellbeing and trying their best to develop a peaceful relationship so they could mutually support Aisha and not be at each other's throats.

"Well, you want to be at each other's somethings anyway," Aisha said dryly. "That much I believe."

Charlie was suddenly exhausted. "You're being ridiculous—and inappropriate. Cut me a break, will you?"

Aisha paused in the middle of unlocking her door and looked up at him, surprised. "Yeah, okay. Sorry. It was just super strange. I don't know Sam. Maybe for her it was just a casual dinner. But I do know you—and I've never seen you look like that or be like that with anyone except Mom. It weirded me out."

"Do you want me to come in for a bit? We could watch TV or play Scrabble. . . ."

Aisha shook her head. "I wasn't just being a jerk when I said I was wiped. I hope I'm not coming down with something."

"No, you definitely are. It's called About-to-birth-itis. Text or call if you need anything." He pressed his lips against Aisha's forehead. "And get some sleep."

Aisha side-hugged him, all her girth would allow. "I'll try. You too."

For the first time in his life that he could recall, Charlie wasn't disappointed his daughter didn't want to hang out.

By the time he got back to the cabin, he was soaked to the skin despite his jacket, the candles had burnt out, and Sam's room was quiet with no light showing beneath the door. He surveyed the congealed remains of their dinner and spent wine and sighed. He'd had a dessert planned and they hadn't even gotten to enjoy it. All the energy he'd felt earlier had drained away completely, but he cleaned everything up and had a long shower before he hit the sack anyway, and still sleep didn't come.

It was good, very good, that Aisha had interrupted them when she had. Wasn't it? But then again, interrupted what? Nothing was really happening—and nothing had happened. And probably nothing more than what she'd witnessed *would have* happened.

He rolled over, punched his pillow and wedged it under his cheek. He was all too aware that just ten feet away, separated by two thin doors and one narrow hall, Samantha lay in bed alone too. Was she awake and thinking of them as well, or was that completely laughable?

Chapter 13

SAM LISTENED TO THE CLINKING dishes as Charles tidied and considered getting up, offering to help, and discussing what had happened between them—except that nothing *had* happened, not really, so what was there to say?

She'd seen the revulsion and near-hatred that flared in Aisha's eyes when she realized Charlie was touching her. The ferocity of her anger seemed over the top—but then again, Sam remembered all too well what she'd thought of the gaggle of men her mom paraded through her and Jo's life. She didn't hate them as much as Jo had—it would've been far smarter and way better for her if she had, actually—but to say she hadn't respected them would've been an understatement. Charles didn't seem like a player, but then again what would she know? Maybe his whole cute, awkward and inexperienced shtick *was* his shtick.

She rolled onto her side and curled into a ball as the kitchen noise ceased and Charlie's feet padded down the hall. Knock on my door, she thought. Say good night or something. He didn't do anything of the sort—just headed into the bathroom. The shower turned on and stayed on for a long time.

No, worse than Aisha's disdain and obvious outrage at the tiny spark of interest between the two of them, was Charlie's response. He'd dropped her feet like they'd turned into snakes and his widened eyes and instant flush said he was just as shocked and unhappy about the scenario as Aisha was.

It was, as ever, Sam decided, a case of too much wine and a woman that seemed available for a time—but not the kind you make yourself available to. Still, she couldn't help imagining him in the shower and daydreaming about those strong hands of his rubbing a couple other areas that could use some attention.

She spent the rest of the night tossing and turning, and finally, when it wasn't too, too early, she let herself get up. She did her hair and makeup quickly, packed a bag with yoga pants and a T-shirt so she could hit Dave's gym, and was out of the house, laptop in hand, before Charlie stirred. She'd eat in town, work for a bit, then hang out with Dave—or call Jo in the afternoon and see if they could meet somewhere for a visit.

She had, against her better judgment she realized now, promised to stay at least until the baby was born. She wondered if Aisha would even want her to now. Ah, well, time would tell.

The next three days passed similarly. She was carefully up before Charlie each morning, and stayed gone until he was in bed. It was tedious, and all the hotels—she called them each daily—were still completely booked.

There was one small bright spot, however. Aisha didn't seem to hate her after all, "cozy" dinner with Charlie notwithstanding, and it surprised her to admit it, but the girl was growing on her too. They were meeting at The Zoo for the fourth day in a row, and as Sam waited, surprise zipped through her. She'd actually miss their visits when they were done.

Maybe Aisha was feeling something similar because as she settled her bulk into her favorite window seat, she didn't bother with a greeting, just launched into talk right away. "It's odd to me that you're, I don't know, so familiar when really we've just met. I mean, you don't feel like my mother or anything—I had a perfectly good mom. I'm not looking for a replacement."

Sam nodded, feeling agreement, relief and the tiniest sliver of what, regret? She wrapped her hands around her mug and took a large sip of her green tea.

"But at the same time, well, there is something there, something between us, that I can't deny. You're more than some stranger I've just met, if that makes sense."

"It does, yeah. It's kind of how I feel, actually."

Aisha studied her. "So I don't feel like your daughter?"

EV BISHOP

"I don't know. Intellectually, I know that's what you are, and the family resemblance still catches me off guard . . . but at the same time, like you said, you had a mother, that role was filled. Hearing you say it so firmly makes me happy—relieved actually. I didn't know much about your parents at all. I made my decision based on their letters and a few references and photos. We never met in person. Adoption wasn't open back then, the way it often is now, and even the bit of choice I demanded on having was considered irregular, but I—" Sam's voice caught a little and she feigned a small cough to mask it, hating her weakness. "I only ever wanted you to have the home I didn't have."

"Well, you succeeded. I had a really good one—or did until the last few years, which have kind of sucked, but that's not your fault or my dad's."

Aisha turned her attention to her cranberry-orange muffin for a minute, and Sam wondered if she should've made a full disclosure instead of opting for the safe half-truth. Absolutely, she was glad Aisha felt she'd had a good life and didn't seem to harbor any bitterness or anger about Sam's choice. She'd done enough reading to know that wasn't always the case in reunion situations. But, maybe especially because she didn't have other children, Sam did feel like Aisha was her daughter. She had, despite all her denial over the years even to herself, always felt a motherly weight of concern and a desire to protect—hence giving Aisha up in the first place. But saying so would only insert awkwardness into their meetings, or, worse, might make Aisha feel like Sam thought Aisha had some obligation to her—or vice versa—and nothing could be further from the truth.

"So . . . " Sam said. "I can't believe you're going to get much bigger or go much longer—"

"Yeah, my doctor says it's normal for first babies to be a bit overdue, but I'm approaching two weeks. If I don't go in naturally this weekend, they'll induce me on Monday."

"And that's okay?"

Aisha shrugged.

"So is it time to have that talk you've been wanting to have?"

They had yet to discuss Aisha's birth father or Sam's thoughts on keeping or not keeping the child, and Aisha didn't pretend to not know what Sam meant.

"Yeah, about that . . . " She sighed heavily. "I think I've already made up my mind—and maybe the reason I didn't have the nerve to ask you directly when I first laid eyes on you was because I already knew what I wanted to do."

Sam nodded and waited.

Aisha toyed with the saltshaker, rolling it back and forth between her palms. The nervous gesture registered with Sam immediately because Aisha usually came across as rock-steady confident. "I'm keeping the bean. Think I always knew I was going to. Am I nuts?"

Sam studied the young face across from hers and

for the first time saw only the ways it was different from her own, not the similarities. "Well, as you pointed out earlier, we just met so I don't know you that well. You definitely could be nuts."

Aisha laughed.

"But you don't *seem* like it," Sam continued. "You seem self-assured and competent."

"So you think I'm making the right decision."

"I don't think you'll regret it, no—but it won't be easy. It means as of the kid's birthday you'll be a full-fledged grown up, in charge of someone else."

Aisha set the saltshaker neatly beside the pepper in the center of the table.

"And you'll need a good job and hopefully an education. It will be a lot of work."

A shadow crossed Aisha's features, then was gone. "I'm on it—and I have enough saved, believe it or not, to live for a full year without income, so long as I keep things simple. And I have lots of support—emotional and financial, though I'd like to take care of us myself if possible."

Sam's shoulders rocked forward in a full body nod. "Sounds like you have it all planned."

They were both quiet for a moment, long-cooled teas forgotten.

"So that's it? No drama, no strong emotion either way?" Aisha asked.

Sam bit her lip, then raised an eyebrow. "What's to be emotional about? You'll do great. And I'm excited to meet her—or him—when the day comes."

Aisha's jaw tightened, but then she reached out and gently patted Sam's hand. Sam was at a bit of a loss as to why—and to what it meant—and felt as uncomfortable and deficient and lacking as she ever had.

"It's been a long day," Aisha said. "Do you mind if we cut our visit short?"

"No, no, of course not."

Sam watched Aisha go her own way, then sat alone for a while. She had no place to go, nowhere to be—and couldn't pretend even to herself she had something to keep her busy—so she went to the drugstore, bought a plethora of magazines about cabin life, RVing, bed-and-breakfasts and the like, then headed back to River's Sigh.

Mercifully there was no sign of Charlie's Toyota, so she didn't have to go and waste Jo's time or bother her with inane chatter. She let herself into Rainbow and went directly to her room. She did not pass Go. She did not collect two hundred dollars. She lay facedown on her bed and did something she knew all too well was useless and that she didn't normally let herself indulge in. She wept. For the daughter she'd given up and the young woman she was getting to know. The one who'd made out okay—and would no doubt go on to great things. The one who'd found herself in the same predicament Sam had, but who'd somehow come through the experience, confidence still intact, knowing and believing she could give a child what it needed to thrive. The one who weighed pros and cons and felt she had options, choices. Who had supports she could casually reference and then say she hoped she didn't need them.

And she cried for the girl she'd used to be—who looked a lot like Aisha, but was different in every way. Sam didn't regret giving Aisha up for adoption, not then and not now, regardless of any maternal twinges she occasionally felt, but she'd also never really considered it a choice—more like the only viable option. And sometimes she had wondered if she'd done the right thing. And now she knew. She absolutely had.

Chapter 14

THE LIGHT WAS ON UNDER Sam's bedroom door. Charlie hesitated in the hallway. He wanted to knock and say he was home, ask if he could get her anything, see how she was faring—but they were nothing to each other, really. He should take the hint. Besides, it was for the best.

He made tea, then headed to the living room and turned on his laptop. It was all too clear from the way Sam avoided the cabin and him at all costs that he wasn't in her way if he worked in the cabin's main space. Why let it go to waste? He lit a fire and got to work. He was midway through chapter two—a new story though. He'd restarted from scratch, saving the original snippets in a folder named "Cutting Room Floor" that he sometimes perused for scenes or characters that might work in later stories.

He'd just found his groove when his phone buzzed. He picked it up, glanced at the phone's face. Aisha.

"Hey, baby girl. How are—"

"Dad." It was Aisha's voice all right, but tenser and

quieter than he'd ever heard it. A huffing sound of exhaled air and stress came over the line. "You should—come. Come now."

"It's okay, Aisha. You're doing great. I'll be right there." Charlie left his stuff in the living room exactly as it lay, grabbed his wallet and keys, shoved his feet into his boots, and ran for Minnow cabin. "I'm almost at your door. Are you able to walk?"

"Yes, yes, of course." She must be between contractions now because her voice was stronger, more Aisha-like.

"Good. Grab your overnight bag"—they'd organized and packed a small suitcase for the hospital together the day after he'd arrived—"and your coat. Meet me on your porch."

She was waiting for him when he got there, bare legged in a nightie, jacket and boots. Just as he climbed the steps, she clutched the banister and bent double, her face pale as skim milk in the light from the exterior bulb above the door. "Oh, Daddy, it hurts—it hurts."

The cold wind and driving rain had kicked up again and Charlie considered moving her back into the house until the worst of the latest contraction passed, but decided against it. Once it subsided, they'd have a few pain-free minutes before the next one hit. He put his arm around her waist, about to help her to the car. Aisha gave a surprised yelp and something wet and heavy hit the ground and splashed his pant legs.

"It's okay. It's just your water breaking," he whispered, praying that it was just her water—then trying not to panic when the coppery scent of blood hit him. Aisha moaned and her fingers pressed so deeply into his arm he thought she might pierce skin. "It's okay," he repeated, willing it to be so. "Things are just moving quickly. Let's go."

It occurred to him as he drove white-knuckled to the hospital that maybe he should've let Sam or Jo know—or maybe not. Maybe he was right to leave notifying them in Aisha's hands, unless she requested differently. Gah, maneuvering the transition from parent of child to parent of adult with a child was going to be rough. The whole experience was like going into a skid on an icy road. You couldn't hit the brakes, needed to keep steering, even apply some gas, but had to be careful not to overcompensate and throw yourself into a spin.

The emergency room's stark fluorescent lights confirmed Charlie's fear. The spill down Aisha's legs wasn't amniotic fluid—or not purely amniotic fluid anyway. Her thighs and calves were streaked a bloody pink, Charlie's pants crimson-spattered. The nurse behind the desk took one look at them, called someone on the intercom, then pushed a wheelchair over to Aisha.

"I'll take her upstairs. You go to admitting and let them know she's here."

"Is everything all right?" Charlie could hardly

breathe.

"Second floor. See you there." The nurse whisked Aisha away, the wheelchair shushing along the bile-yellow industrial flooring like even the stupid chair was telling him to shut up.

Thank goodness, Aisha had taken the doctor's advice and visited the hospital and signed in ahead of time with all her info. It really was just a matter of saying she'd arrived. In five minutes Charlie was upstairs, pulling a blue gown over his clothes, donning a shower cap like hat, and sliding elastic banded fabric slippers over his shoes. He fought the fear, hopelessness and sadness that the smell of the ward sent coursing through him. He hated the stink of hospitals. The scent of death wasn't the rank aroma of decomposition; it was the antiseptic cleaners of hospital hallways. He hated the overly bright, cheerless light too.

When he got into her room, Aisha was already sporting her own hospital gown and a variety of wires and cords were fed into her body. She looked about twelve, but her color was better. In between body wracking pains, she kept trying to joke. It was driving him crazy.

A nurse came over and told him what he'd already guessed. Aisha's water had broken, and yes, there was blood in the mix. Unlike him, however, the nurse wasn't concerned. Apparently a flow of fresh blood, coming away all at once, was normal for some women at the end of the first stage of labor—exactly where Aisha seemed to be, as her cervix was very soft and quite dilated. They'd attached a heartbeat monitor to Aisha's belly, and baby seemed fine. No distress. They'd notified the doctor Aisha had seen in Greenridge and he was conveniently already on site doing his evening rounds. He'd check on her as soon as he finished.

Charlie hadn't chewed his nails since he was a teenager, so he was startled to find himself worrying away at a rough corner of his thumb with his teeth. He shoved his hands into his pockets, trying desperately to avoid thinking of Maureen—pre-cancer, pre her ever being sick, in those awful years when they'd tried and tried to have their own biological children and she miscarried and miscarried and miscarried, the last and final time at a devastating six months. Nowadays their little girl would likely have lived—

His thoughts flew to his living, breathing daughter. Please God, don't take her, he thought. Don't take either of them. Please God. *Please*.

Parents shouldn't be in the labor room with their children, he thought still later, after being informed by a somewhat impatient nurse that Aisha was fine—young and healthy and having a "perfect" labor. This was perfect? It went against every fiber of his being to see her in so much pain. "Maybe you should consider the epidural before it's too late."

A look to kill flashed in Aisha's eyes—eyes so

alight and focused on her purpose that they seemed to burn.

"Okay, so no drugs yet, but at least consider it . . . if you need them, right?"

A rapid panting breath. "Most parents want their kids off drugs, Dad."

"Har, har—look, is there anything I can do for you?"

"Yeah, get away from me. You're driving me crazy."

The nurse checking Aisha's vitals smothered a smile, and Charlie scowled. This was serious business. They shouldn't be taking it so damn lightly. He sighed and paced to the window—then felt gratitude that Aisha had gone into labor when she had. The sky was dumping every kind of weather you could imagine all at once. The trees glittered black and icy under the streetlights and were bent almost in half by the assaulting wind. The parking lot was a slough of slushy snow and water. A car barreled through and literally left a wake behind it.

"Dad?" Aisha's voice. Conciliatory. "You don't really drive me crazy. Usually."

He turned, smiling—and remembered how he and Mo used to wonder which one of them she'd inherited her wit and occasional razor sharpness from. Now, so often when Aisha talked, Sam's face popped into his mind. And he'd only known the woman a few weeks.

There was a flurry of activity and whispers by the

118

bedside. One of the nurses said she'd call. Call who? Charlie wanted to know. Aisha moaned, falling into a crevice of deep pain, when mere seconds earlier she'd been fine. Charlie's guts churned with dread. He hated this waiting. These pauses of calm peace, shattered by excruciating anxiety.

"I wish Mom was here," Aisha wheezed, then moaned again.

Charlie's heart squeezed.

"Can . . . can you call Sam? Please."

Charlie froze. "Absolutely. Are you sure?"

Aisha nodded once. Her voice was an exhaled whoosh. "Yes. Am sure."

He conferred with the nurses. They figured Aisha was progressing "nicely" and was close to delivering. They'd alerted the doctor that it wouldn't be long. Yet they still insisted he had time to make phone calls.

The smile-smothering nurse practically shoved him from the room. "Even if she starts pushing, it's her first and she's young. It won't be a quick process."

Charlie's hands shook and he sat down in one of the blue vinyl chairs outside Aisha's room, instead of making the call standing up. He checked his phone for the time before dialing. It was only 8:00 p.m.—a fact that flummoxed him. It was the strangest thing. It felt like it should be the middle of the night or something.

Jo answered on the first ring. "Hey, Jo. Charlie here. Do you have Sam's cell number, by chance?"

There was a pause, then a cautious, "Of course . . .

what's up?"

Charlie wasn't sure what to say. Aisha had in-structed him to call Sam, but he doubted she'd care if Jo knew, too. Besides Sam would probably tell her sister anyhow. "Nothing serious—or nothing serious-bad, I mean. Aisha's in labor. At the hospital. She wanted—"

Jo interrupted, rattling off a number so quickly he had to ask for it again. Realizing he'd forgotten to grab notepaper, he wrote it on his hand as she repeated it.

He dialed Sam's number the moment he and Jo disconnected.

Sam's voice was groggy. "Hello?"

"Sam?"

"At your service."

"It's Charlie."

"So?"

So? What the hell kind of response was *so*?

"Charlie?"

"Yeah, yeah—I'm here. At the hospital. It's Aisha. She's in labor. It's pretty rough." Pretty rough? That was the wrong thing to say. She'd totally freak out.

"Rough how?"

"Er . . . hard to watch your kid go through that kind of pain."

There was a second of silence and he sensed she nodded. He pushed on. "She asked me to call you."

"Really? Why?"

Charlie shook his head. Why indeed? It was anyone's guess. "I think she'd like you to come . . . if you can, if it's not too much trouble."

The sound of a rapid exhale filled his ear, then a rushed, "Yes, yes, of course. Does she need anything? Or do you? Can I bring something? Should I?"

"No, no—just yourself." Before he could add another word, she said good-bye and ended the call.

Samantha strode into hospital hallway, where Charlie sat waiting for her as per Aisha's request. She was there so quickly, he shuddered to think how fast she'd driven, then was momentarily taken aback by what she was wearing. Yoga pants. A thick eggshell blue hooded sweatshirt. *Running shoes.*

She flicked her ponytail over her shoulder and shrugged. "Yeah, I know. It's a terrible outfit—but I don't want to get baby gunk on my good shoes."

He chuckled, but it was cut short by a worried-looking nurse and a hurrying doctor who dashed into Aisha's room without giving him or Samantha a glance.

"Just a second."

Sam nodded and he bolted for the room, too—only to be shooed out. "There's a bit of a complication, Mr. Bailey."

"No, no, there's not. They assured me, they told us, me and my daughter—everything's going fine. Everything's good."

"Unfortunately, there's been a bit of a development, but there's no need to panic."

The words, of course, sent a zip line of that exact emotion—panic—racing through Charlie. Sam closed the distance between herself and him, standing close but not quite touching.

"The umbilical cord is wrapped around the baby's neck. It's common—happens in almost one in three deliveries—and usually isn't a serious complication, but the baby's big and Aisha has a narrow pelvis. Her contractions aren't as effective as we'd like, and the fetal heartbeat has dropped. We're booking an emergency C-section to be proactive."

"Can I accompany her, for . . . support?" Charlie could barely get the words out.

"Normally, yes—but they're moving in a hurry. Let me go and chat with the doctor who's prepping her and I'll let you know."

Chapter 15

HOW LONG HAD IT BEEN, minutes, hours? Sam had no idea. She perched rigidly on the edge of an ancient, ugly blue chair beside Charlie and tried to distract herself with thoughts about how the dingy dump that called itself a hospital desperately needed an upgrade.

The halls looked like the aftermath of a garage sale for obsolete equipment. Old beds lined the walls, piled high with folded bedding. (God, they didn't really use bedding that was stored open in the hallway, did they?) Wheeled contraptions with paint-peeling oxygen tanks that looked circa World War Two sat in depressive huddles. A janitor cart with an overflowing waste bucket on one end and three tiers of gray plastic bins full of dirty dishes and discarded food jutted out at an angle from the wall, creating a germ-breeding night-mare, an eyesore, and a tripping hazard all in one genius move.

She did everything in her power to avoid thinking about how Charlie's hand had gripped her knee when the nurse told him they thought it was better for him to wait here until Aisha was out of surgery. And she tried to fight her hyper-awareness of that same hand, resting in hers now, their fingers interlocked.

His heartbeat pulsed against her flesh where their wrists touched. It had been rapid fire at first, but had slowed a little now—

Oh yeah, she was doing a marvelous job "fighting her awareness" of Charles Bailey. *Just marvelous.*

Directly across from where they sat, but about twelve feet off the floor, hung a round-faced clock, like the ones Samantha remembered from school. Black-framed, white-faced, with a long arrow for the hour hand, a shorter arrow for a minute hand and a skinny red arrow to tick out each second. The time crept along slowly, but audibly. A metronome of anxiety.

She cast a sideways glance at Charles just as he looked her way—and, he, ever the stalwart champ, tried to smile. She squeezed his hand and returned the smile, hoping hers wasn't as feeble an attempt at reassurance as his was. She had no idea about the risks or possibilities of a good outcome when labor went wrong. She'd spent her one and only experience with pregnancy, carrying Aisha, in denial, gaining as little as possible, though making sure she stayed within what wouldn't hurt the baby's development, and wearing control top pantyhose.

She'd given birth in six hours from start to finish and checked herself out of the hospital within twenty-four hours, preferring to huddle on her uncle's couch in front of the TV with a huge container of ibuprofen and snacks (even way back then, Ray's place had been too much of hoarder's hell for her to have her own room—and Jo stayed there more often than she did, so she had dibs). She pretended she was enduring the world's worst period and hadn't just had a kid. After forty-two hours she called her mom, got an answering machine and left a terse message. "You can stop worrying. Everything went fine." Which was hilarious now that she thought about it. Like her mom had ever worried.

Charlie shifted beside her and she thudded back to the present, her cheeks burning. Thinking about her own sorry past did not help Aisha.

Sam didn't notice she was rubbing slow gentle circles along Charlie's fingers with her thumb until he turned sideways in his seat to face her. She stopped abruptly, mortified, and started to pull her hand away.

Charlie tightened his grip, and his eyes locked on hers. "No, don't stop. It helps."

If her body temperature was any indicator, Sam knew her face was fuchsia. She couldn't free her hand now unless she tugged hard—and worse, she didn't really *want* to free it. Holding hands helped her too, and though she knew full well that Charlie was only taking comfort from her because she was there—that it wasn't personal—for the time being it didn't matter. When was the last time she'd held hands with a boy anyway? A long time obviously—considering she'd thought "boy" instead of man.

She sighed and Charlie looked concerned, so she forced another smile, relaxed her fingers and continued the soothing-to-them-both circles.

How long did it take to extract one tiny infant? Good grief.

It was almost midnight when the Maternity ward door banged open, making them both jump. Shift had changed and an unfamiliar nurse with short black hair and pink cheeks strode toward them.

They dropped hands. Stood.

"I have excellent news," the nurse said, beaming. "Aisha's doing great, and if you want to wash up and put on fresh gowns, there's a robust little someone anxious to meet you."

Samantha's knees went weak, and she almost buckled under the weight and the relief the words carried. "You—you go," she said. "I don't want to intrude. Tell Aisha . . . congratulations."

"No, you're coming too. Aisha asked for you, and she'll want you to meet the baby. I know Aisha. She'll be proud as punch and will want *everyone* to meet the baby."

The nurse's grin broadened. "Yes, she's a fire-cracker, that one. Even in the middle of surgery, she was asking questions—and she insisted on not having a curtain. She watched the whole procedure."

Ugh. That sounded beyond hideous. "I don't know—"

"You're coming." Charlie's hand was on her again, this time on her forearm. How she hated that his smallest touch warmed every part of her.

"*Fine*," she said grouchily. The nurse shot her a surprised look. Charlie just smiled.

Aisha's room and hospital bed were empty, and Sam looked around uncertainly. Maybe they'd misunderstood where they were supposed to go?

A different nurse bustled in, a bundle of butter-yellow flannel in her arms. Sam caught sight of a miniature face—red and furious with a tiny rosebud mouth—and inhaled sharply.

"Mr. and Mrs. Bailey, meet your granddaughter."

Sam looked at Charlie, but he was staring at the little girl, enrapt, and didn't correct the nurse—maybe didn't even hear her. And Sam didn't care. It was so nice to pretend she belonged to this sweet family scene, even just for a moment—and he was letting her.

The nurse held the child out to Sam. She stepped back, right into Charlie's firm body.

"Take her," he said softly.

And Sam did. Oh-so-gingerly, heart hammering in her chest, she reached out and took the first baby she'd held in seventeen years into her arms.

"Hey there, little one. Hello," Charlie crooned. Sam didn't say a word. Just stared and stared. This tiny little creature carried her blood, and in a strange and wonderful way—albeit one she wasn't arrogant enough to take any credit for—existed, sort of, because of her. It was mind-blowing.

Samantha lowered her face to the baby and breathed in. A flood of memories rushed back to her, memories she'd never really let herself focus on. Oh, it was going to be hard to leave all this behind. What had she done? She never should've agreed to meet Aisha—to come here. She should have stuck to her old plan.

The baby returned her study, wide-eyed and solemn, with that excruciating see-through-you wisdom babies sometimes seemed to possess. When do we lose that? Sam wondered. Wisdom would be nice about now. The thought startled her.

The baby yawned, then turned its head and made a sucking motion with its mouth. "Your turn," Sam whispered. She was just about to pass the baby off when another nurse came into the room. "Your wife looks young enough to be the mama, not the grandma."

Charlie's eyes locked on Sam's again and for a second time, he didn't bother to correct the nurse. Just smiled, his chocolate eyes soft with warmth and kindness. "Prettiest grandma I ever saw," he said.

Sam's heart—corny as it was, she berated herself—seemed to go pitter-pat. He was so silly and kind, but he was also right. She was a grandma. Beyond bizarre. For the first time since Aisha had arrived back in Sam's life, she let the question in. *What if.* What if Aisha would let Sam be a continued part of her life in some capacity? Sam tried to stamp out that spark of hope, knowing all too well that only pain and rejection lay down that path of thinking, but it was too late. The yearning had articulated itself and now sat like a burning coal at the back of her throat.

Charlie held the impossibly tiny human and Sam had to glance away. She couldn't handle the expression that blanketed his face and moistened his eyes. Love. That was the only thing you could call it. Pure, unadulterated love. For the second time in two days, Sam felt her choice to give up Aisha solidly affirmed—even as her heart ached for all the things she'd never had.

Chapter 16

RAINBOW CABIN WAS AGLOW WHEN Charlie rolled into his usual parking spot in the wee hours of dawn. Kind of Sam, he thought, to think to leave lights on for him. She'd left half an hour or so after Aisha came back to the room, but he'd stayed to visit longer, both of them falling asleep intermittently, then waking when the baby stirred. Aisha was in love with her child, anyone could see it, and Charlie had felt his own questions fade away.

He would always respect—and appreciate to a depth words couldn't express—people who carried babies to term and chose adoption for their children— but in this case . . . Aisha's case, *their family's case* . . . keeping little Mo—a.k.a. Maureen Katriana Bailey-Brown (quite a mouthful for one little girl!) felt infinitely right. Not that it would always be easy, but he suspected the reverse was true as well: letting someone else raise your child might be right, but it was no doubt difficult as hell in some ways too. He thought of the expression that kissed Sam's face when she first looked down at Mo. Completely unguarded. She wasn't the hard case she liked to pretend she was. Far from it, he suspected. Maybe the furthest thing from it.

He was smiling as he opened the door, then jolted with happy surprise when a blanketed bump on the couch shifted. Sam had waited up for him.

"Hey there, gramps," she whispered, her voice craggy with disuse. Ice tinkled in a glass. When he pulled off his shoes and walked closer, he smelled hard alcohol. "Quite the day, hey?" She wasn't quite slurring, but it was accurate to say her words had no sharp edges.

He sank onto the small couch beside her and felt heat coming off her body, a direct contrast to the chill he still carried from outdoors.

She looked at him. He looked at her. "Drinking alone?" he asked.

"Not anymore," she quipped, then winked. "How do you like your bourbon?"

"I'm not sure, uh—"

"A bourbon virgin? How sweet!" Sam popped up and practically skipped to the fridge, her drink not so much as sloshing. For crying out loud, even tanked she moved with an agility and grace that made most people seem clumsy.

More ice clanked, liquid poured, something fizzed—but whatever bottles she was planning to poison him with were hidden from view by the fridge. She was back a second later, handing him a glass. He looked at the light golden beverage then up at her.

"It's good. You'll like it."

He sipped tentatively. Then took a larger, more appreciative drink. "It is good. I *do* like it."

"Told you," she said, looking down at him with lowered lashes. She swayed side to side, not drunkenly, but like she was considering something.

"What?"

"Nothing." She plunked back down and he noticed her own drink had been topped up. "Cheers," she said and raised a toast. "It's not every day you get a new granddaughter."

"Cheers," he replied and clinked his glass to hers. The heavy cut crystal made a pretty sound.

"Are you totally exhausted?" she asked.

"Er . . . not totally."

"Good, let's celebrate till the sun comes up—which might be a long time in this godforsaken hellhole they call a valley."

Charles laughed—but for some reason he couldn't explain even to himself, he felt a little weepy. He clutched his glass in both hands. "Sounds good." His crazy jag of emotions must've left a tear in his voice or something because Samantha turned to him and her gorgeous eyes narrowed.

"What?" she asked.

"Nothing, it's nothing—" but wouldn't you know it, his stupid voice kind of broke.

She set her glass on the coffee table, then did the

weirdest thing. She wrapped her hands around his, which still encircled his drink. "It's okay. Like I said, we had a big day. There was a lot to process."

Tears came. Big ones. They seeped from the corners of his eyes and tracked down his face—and her hands were still pressed to his. He couldn't yank away, blot them out, deny them.

"I . . . " He shook his head. "I . . . can't go the hospital without thinking about death. Maureen and I lost so many babies and then she died—and then Aisha had such a hard time . . . I was sure, I was sure she was . . ."

"Shhh," Samantha said, sounding almost angry. She squeezed her eyes shut for a second and when she opened them, they were different: softer, almost glistening. "I know what it's like to experience bad things and to expect the worst, but it can be a self-fulfilling prophecy." Charlie didn't have time to think about what she meant because she rushed on. "Aisha didn't die—and it sounds like you and I were the only ones who were even worried she would. She's strong, physically and emotionally, and that's thanks to you and Maureen." Sam's voice lowered. "And Charlie—you didn't die either."

She dropped his hands, turned away and picked up her beverage. Took a big drink. "And the kid—little Mo, I mean. She seems pretty durable too."

Charlie sipped the amber concoction in his glass and when he spoke next, his voice was rough even to his own ears. "And what about you, Samantha Kendall? Is that what you are? Durable?"

Samantha's answer, a whisper though it was, pierced him like blade. "I think the word you're looking for is hard, Charlie. *Hard*." She grinned then, like she was trying to pass the comment off as a joke, but he wasn't fooled.

He wanted to deny it, to say something to encourage her the way she had him, but Samantha settled deeper into the couch and rested her head against his shoulder. Charlie's brain—and all thoughts—stuttered to a stop.

He breathed in the scent of her hair and the boozy, fading fragrance of her perfume—of her. The slight weight of her body against his felt like it was imprinting on him for life. He let out a deep exhale. What had she said? He wasn't dead yet.

A couple drinks later, conversation and the mood had swung full circle, maybe become a bit manic. They talked about music. She had terrible taste, was totally stuck in the eighties and it made him howl.

"Well, at least my playlist doesn't look like it belongs to a thirteen-year-old girl," she said with feigned indignation.

"That'd be insulting—except it *was* probably created by a thirteen-year-old girl. Aisha used to be obsessed with fooling around with my phone and I haven't updated either, the music or the device, for almost five years."

"And you say I'm stuck in some outdated generation."

They both laughed.

They talked about food.

"Dinner with you the other night—that's the first meal I've cooked that hasn't come out of a box in . . . years," he admitted. He'd been about to say since his wife died, but for once he didn't want to bring Maureen into the conversation.

"And that's the first time I've eaten that many carbs in one sitting in years *and* years."

Ah, so that's what lay behind her initial hesitation to eat that night. Silliness. "You don't need to watch what you eat. You look amazing."

Sam's eyebrow quirked and her lips twitched. "Yes—because I don't eat carbs. With great legs comes great responsibility."

"What—*no*! Tell me you did not just completely butcher a Spiderman quote and make it about your body?"

Samantha stretched and Charlie was all the more conscious of the body about which they spoke.

"My *great* body you mean? And sure, why not? Poetic license—that's a thing right?"

"Well, I'm going to feed you nothing but carbs."

Sam laughed. "No way. It's my turn to cook next. Canned soup it is."

And they started to discuss work. Samantha wanted to dig into his writing process in great detail and was dissatisfied by his comment, "The biggest part of my process is that I rarely speak of my process."

"That's a cop-out."

He shrugged.

"No, seriously. There's got to be something you can tell me. How did you get into writing romance anyway? I know you're not the only guy who does, but it's not the most common thing either."

His pause gave her all the encouragement she needed to push harder. She squealed a little. "Wait, wait—this is going to be good. I know it. Let me get another drink." She refilled both their cups generously, then sat down cross-legged on the floor in front of him and looked up expectantly. She was just so damn cute.

He shook his head again. "Fine, but it'll sound dumb."

"Perfect. I'm all ears."

"No, no, you're all something, but it's definitely not ears."

"Heh," she said. "Don't change the subject."

Charles swirled the contents of his glass, creating a little whirlpool of ice, ginger ale and bourbon. "I used to tell Maureen . . . stories."

"You used to tell your wife stories . . ." Sam repeated—then squealed, "Ah! You mean like *foreplay stories*?"

Heat flooded every one of Charlie's limbs. "Oh, yes," he said thickly, assuming his heaviest fake accent. "Very hot, very sexy, I assure you."

Sam arched a perfect brow and with just as much exaggeration, licked her lower lip. "Ooh la la—that hot, that sexy, you say."

Somehow when she said it, equally cheesy or not, it was also . . . crazily, well, exactly those two things: hot and sexy. His pulse pounded.

"And then a little of this led to a little of that?" she asked, placing a finger on his knee and trailing it up the inside seam of his jeans about six inches. His whole body—yep, he was that transparent—stiffened like he was a horny kid. Then again, on some level, maybe everyone was a horny kid forever.

She grinned knowingly. "I mean story-wise, of course."

"Yeah," he croaked. "Of course."

Her grin broadened and his hormones surged.

The room around them was slowly lightening as dawn developed into full-fledged morning, but he wasn't tired at all. He wanted the strange evening-slash-day to last and last. Yep, he was enjoying himself all right—maybe too much. He didn't feel like he had a lick of restraint left, but still managed to redirect. "But what about you?" He waved ambiguously toward the world outside the window. "It's obvious you make decent money—or have decent money. What do you do for a living?"

Samantha sipped her drink and he marveled how despite the hour and the drinks that he could no longer count, she didn't seem any more or less tipsy than when he'd arrived. "Boring," she said.

"Not to me. I want to know."

She considered that and nodded slowly. "I'm an investor of sorts. I'll tell you more eventually—and you'll be bored as promised—but let's not change the other subject just yet."

She was still sitting on the floor, but had moved even closer to the couch. Given his position, legs apart, feet planted, she was practically framed by his knees. And she was definitely leaning in and even more definitely flirting. A rush of giddiness made him chuckle. Maureen used to always accuse him of being dense—said women flirted with him constantly at conventions and the like but that he never noticed, that it was part of his "charm." She wasn't the jealous type though—or maybe she was, but she just knew he had eyes only for her. Now he felt a bit proud as he formed the thought. *She's flirting with me, Maureen. She definitely is. I can tell.*

Well, holy cow and cue the orchestra. She sure is, stud. Go for it, came back Maureen's voice in his head, followed by her musical laugh. For the second time that night, he felt a little teary. Maureen was gone and he'd mourned her a long time. She was okay with him moving on. Maybe. Holy shit—the thought slammed through him—he was hammered.

He lost himself in Sam's eyes and cleavage again. Wondered if she knew he could see right down her shirt from his vantage point—then felt sure, yes, she absolutely knew—and he liked that about her. Her mixture of coquettish games and bluntness. (Not a bad title for a romance short, actually . . . *Coquettish Games and Bluntness*.)

All he wanted to do was pull her up to standing and—

"Now, Mr. Bailey, whatever are you thinking?" she asked, but the little glint in her eyes and the way her tongue touched her lower lip for just a second told him she knew exactly *what*. She stood, topped their glasses once more with a bottle that had made its way to the floor beside her—but then placed both drinks just out of reach on the coffee table and stepped close, straddling one of his outstretched legs.

He contained a moan, but barely. She really was *so* hot. And it had been such an amazing day. He wasn't himself, or the self he tried to be anyway, when he reached up and gripped her hips, then guided her onto his lap.

"Oh," she purred, placing her hands on his shoulders. They considered each other for what seemed a long time. Out the window, just beyond Samantha, the sun was making an appearance now, peeking through the charcoal clouds, rendering them gold and silver. A surreal light spilled through the window in visual rays and gave Samantha's hair a glowing halo-like effect.

Charlie stroked one finger down her velvet-soft skin from temple to cheek.

She smiled down at him and leaned in. Her breath

tickled his face and sometime recently she'd partaken of a breath mint or something because an intoxicating scent of spearmint mingled with the sweetness of bourbon. He wanted to taste her.

"Here's what I propose," she said.

"Propose? But lady, I hardly know you."

"Ha ha, funny man." But the skin around her eyes crinkled into those lines he'd already learned to watch for—the true cue to her mood despite her signature dry tone. All he wanted to do was make her eyes laugh all the time.

She bent in so close her lips were almost touching his. His clamp on her hips tightened. "As I was saying," she whispered, her voice mostly air. "I propose we stop pretending we don't both want the same thing. Let's have our fling, make it really good, and get it out of our systems."

If she'd literally thrown a bucket of ice water over him, Charlie's libido—or his mental libido anyway—couldn't have been more instantly or thoroughly extinguished.

"What?" He could hardly formulate words. His body still wanted what it wanted, but his mind reeled.

"Oh, come on . . ." Her voice was still sultry and seductive and her hand teased along his jaw and down his chest. "The kids are away, the adults can play."

He wanted to play. He really did. But dammit, he already felt his desire wilting. He knew himself too well. He'd never been the guy for light games. And

Sam . . . He stared at her hard and she flinched and straightened, though remained on his lap.

He recalled her earlier comment about being "hard."

"Such bullshit," he muttered sadly.

"What?" Her posture went even more rigid. "What is it?"

His head was a muddle of regret and he hadn't even squeezed the words out. "I'm sorry, Sam—and so lame, but this, I mean, you, me . . . I want to, but—"

"But *what*?" She was half standing now, perched for flight.

"Just we're both so drunk and we had such an intense day. I really . . . like you—and I'd like to . . . just not like this."

Her green eyes speared him. "Oh my God," she said. "You're serious? So what, you thought we'd make love-sweet-love and last forever?"

"No . . . " He shook his head but wondered if maybe that wasn't exactly what he'd been thinking.

Samantha bolted to her feet, but remained so close he could still feel heat emanating from her. "Last chance, Bailey."

"Sam . . ."

She grimaced in disgust. "Oh, fuck you. Forget it."

She was halfway to her room when she stormed back, grabbed her still-full glass and the almost empty bottle and raised them both in another toasting gesture. "To romance and real life working out great." And then she was gone.

Charles lifted his own lonely drink and raised it to the empty room. Its melting ice cubes slinked around the brim, too far gone to make a cheery clink. "Hear, hear," he said.

A moment later he got up and dumped the untouched beverage down the kitchen sink.

Chapter 17

SAM SLEPT RESTLESSLY AND HAD half-dozing dreams that replayed bad memories over and over again. It was an irony she often faced when she drank too much: she drank to forget, but then it wrecked her ability to sleep deeply—the only time she truly did forget.

"So why do you drink so much then, you fucking drunk?" she muttered at one point, flipping her pillow. Unfortunately she couldn't let herself off the hook so easily. Addictions were compulsive, uncontrollable. Her drinking was neither of those things, not really. She wasn't an alcoholic. She was all too aware when she was going to hit it hard—and knew all the reasons she chose to, too. Go her! Sometimes it was to give her the excuse to do things she wouldn't while sober. Liquid nerve, right? Sometimes it was because it was easier to be alone with herself while drunk than sober. Sometimes it was just because she got so damned sad. . . . And tonight's fiasco with Charlie? Well, it was probably all three things working together in a lovely head-fucked trio. Would she ever stop being so pathetic? Maybe after she turned forty—which left her a few good years to imbibe. Heh.

She rubbed herself lightly, but it didn't do the trick. She wanted a man. No, she was in her own head so she might as well be truthful. She wanted Charlie—though who knew why. Self-righteous-smug-asshole-jerk. Even in the cool bedroom, her face ignited thinking of her needy come-on and his quick, decisive rejection.

Her hand rested on her freshly groomed mons—what a waste!—and she sighed. She wasn't an idiot. She knew herself and she knew men. Charlie found her attractive, maybe at least as attractive as she found him, so what was his problem? Since when did being drunk rule out a good roll in the hay? If anything, it was the other way around.

At some sleepless midmorning point she was aware of slight noises outside her room and in the hallway—the kind of sounds people make when they're trying too hard to be quiet. Then the outside door opened and shut. Charlie was gone. No doubt off to see Aisha and little Mo. That made her sad.

She lay on her back, tucked the sheet and duvet around herself as tightly as she could, and managed to sleep and stave off thought for a while at least.

The sky was a dull, heavy gray and the clock read 4:04 p.m. when she next opened her eyes. Her mouth felt like something had died in it and her body was leaden.

She listened. Not a sound from any other part of

the house. She decided to risk getting up and bee-lined for the washroom.

She peed, slugged down a glass of water and two ibuprofen, and headed toward her room—just as a surprised voice made her jump.

"Oh, you're awake."

Charlie appeared out of nowhere, awkwardly blocking her way in the hall. She was suddenly all too aware of what she was wearing. Not very fricken much.

"Er, yeah," she said.

His eyes did a quick, involuntary scan of her body, and she watched his expression change and him grow agitated as he realized what he'd just done. She fought the urge to cross her arms over her chest and consciously shifted instead, so her pajama shirt stretched open just that little bit further.

"I visited Aisha and the baby again after I napped," he said.

"I figured."

"It's snowing really hard."

She shook her head. "I don't care. I'm going back to bed."

He reached out and caught her arm. She glared down at his fingers. He turned bright pink and released her.

She was practically panting and felt a little bad for being snappish, but what did he expect? Mixed messages or what? She'd made it perfectly clear he could have her. He'd declined. Sucked to be him.

Back in her room, door firmly closed, she fired off a quick message to Jo, asking if she could do a coffee later that night because she'd done what she'd said she would and was planning to blast off soon. No answer came back right away, which wasn't unusual. Jo checked her phone once or twice a day max.

As she pulled her blankets up to her chin again, she heard the rhythmic tick-tick-tick of fingers rapidly clicking away at a keyboard.

It was the perfect white noise for sleeping, she thought, letting herself enjoy the luxury of drifting off to homey sounds one final time. It really was too bad her and Charlie were parting ways sooner rather than later.

She wasn't sure what woke her, but awaken she did. The light was strange: blue gray but bright some- how, and the window seemed shuttered. What the—

Sam got out of bed, walked over to the opaque glass and pressed her hand against it. It was cold to her touch, and though her handprint appeared in the moisture raised by her warm palm, the yard outside the window remained whited out—literally. Beyond weird.

She pulled her robe on over her sleep shirt, left her bedroom, and strode to the living room. Again the weird light and void of sound. Maybe it was the silence that had woken her—not that she ever would've thought she'd miss Greenridge's almost non-stop barrage of wind and rain and dripping water noises.

There was a reason Jo and Callum had chosen the pretty-if-overly-romantic name "River's Sigh" for their bed-and-breakfast: you could normally hear the nearby river wherever you were on the property, inside or out.

She moved toward the front door and reached for the handle.

"I wouldn't do that, if I were you," Charlie said from behind her—but too late. The door was open and Sam was staring at a solid wall of white, complete with an imprint of the door.

She stood stock still, shocked. "Is that for real? All that's *snow*?"

"Well, yeah. Surreal, hey?"

She hardly heard him. The smell—how frozen precipitation had its own fragrance she'd never understand, but it did—along with the blue-white brightness and separation from the rest of the world triggered a memory she didn't even know she had.

She stepped back, shaking her head, and just narrowly avoided Charlie's bare feet.

"Sorry," she said.

"You look oddly happy for a woman trapped inside a cabin by a wall of snow. What gives?"

Sam shrugged. "Just remembered something from when I was a kid."

"Oh, yeah? What?" Charlie leaned in a little, like he was genuinely eager for whatever she was going to say next.

She shook her head. "It's silly."

"Most really good things are, at least a little bit."

"I made an igloo once, with real ice blocks and everything." Saying it aloud brought the day back with more detail. "My uncle—Ray—he worked for two days straight cutting ice out of the lake for me. I slept overnight in it. I felt like fairy princess crossed with a warrior chief-queen."

Charlie reached out and tucked a strand of her hair behind her ear, his eyes squinting with a smile. "I bet you were something exactly like that—just like now."

A lump formed in the back of Sam's throat though she couldn't have explained why. She backed away a step, but his eyes continued to hold hers. "Your uncle sounds pretty great," he added.

"Yeah, in some ways, I guess maybe he was." Sam heard the surprise in her voice and it increased the tension that suddenly filled her belly. She never talked about her childhood and this was why. She hated it. The confusing happy memory was ruined as quickly as it started.

Charlie reached out, then appeared to think better of touching her. "Are you all right?"

Sam shook her head. "Yeah, sure, of course. Why?" She moved toward the kitchen. The stove's clock read 7:05. Was that a.m. or p.m.? Surely she hadn't gone to bed yesterday afternoon and slept all the way through until now, but then again. . . . That was a monstrous amount of snow, impossible for just a few hours. Good grief.

"Is it morning?" she asked.

"Yep, if you can believe it."

She shook her head. "No, I really can't. I slept for what, fifteen hours?"

"Guess your body needed it."

"Hmmpf. What my body needs is—" *you*, her stupid brain—always the comedian—intoned. Thankfully she hadn't finished the thought out loud.

"Is?" Charlie prompted.

"Caffeine." Sam grabbed a filter from the cabinet above the coffee maker and waved it for emphasis.

"Are you still mad at me?" he asked a second later.

Really? They were going to have this conversation? How perfect. She filled the coffee pot with water and dumped it into the machine, then hit the grind button. Over the roaring of the motor, she said, "Not at all."

"Really?"

The grinding was finished all too soon. Sam hit brew. "Really. And I wasn't so much as angry as I was humiliated. But thanks for bringing it up. Nothing better in the morning than facing all my regrets."

He chuckled but it sounded forced. Great. Why on earth hadn't she just gone to bed after she got home from the hospital last night instead of waiting up? Now she'd ruined everything, just when they'd started to be normal around each other—actually, no, she wasn't taking the full blame. *They'd* wrecked it.

She doctored a mug for herself, then held up an

empty one and shook it in Charlie's direction.

"Sure, please. Just milk."

"I know."

She handed him a full cup a moment later and moved toward the couch with hers.

"I just don't get . . . why are you humiliated? You have nothing to be ashamed of."

"Charlie, can we just avoid this whole conversation?"

"Why?"

"Fine. I, like probably any and every person alive, don't like getting mixed signals, deciding to go for it, then being shot down."

"Is that what you think happened?"

She took a big mouthful of coffee and swallowed slowly. "That *is* what happened."

"May I?" He'd been standing awkwardly with his cup beside the couch and now he motioned at the cushion beside her.

"Be my guest."

He sat down and stared down at his mug. His mouth opened, but whatever he was going to say was cut off by the cabin's shrill landline.

Sam reached for the cordless phone on the end table. "Hello?"

"Sam, thank goodness. You're all right?"

"Of course, I'm all right. We're both all right. It's just snow."

"It's not just snow. Have you seen it out there? It's

a freak show."

"Deep breaths, Jo, deep breaths."

"*You're* telling *me* to take deep breaths?"

"Ironic, isn't it?"

There was a pause on the other end of the line. Then Jo laughed. "Okay, so you're fine. Good. I admit I was worried."

"Are we actually snowed in-snowed in? Like totally trapped?"

"What do you mean?"

"Well, my bedroom window is a blanket of white and the front door, when you open it, is literally a wall of snow."

"Yikes. Callum or I will be over shortly. We got close to four feet of snow, but it's the drifting followed by freezing rain that really did us in. Everything's covered in a shell."

"Okay, so I have just one question."

"Yeah?"

"Why on earth would you willingly choose to live here?"

Jo sighed. "Just relax and don't try to go anywhere. It's an ice rink. Warmer weather is on its way, however. This was winter's big farewell."

"More like winter's big kiss your ass."

"Nice, Sam. I'll talk to you soon."

"Rescue the other bed-and-ice-fest dwellers first."

"I will."

Sam ended the call and resumed sipping her coffee.

Charlie had apparently gleaned enough from her side of conversation that he didn't have any questions—or else he was just a glutton for awkward moments because he continued where they'd left off.

"I didn't shoot you down."

Sam raised her eyebrows.

He set his mug down on the coffee table. "Every bit of me wanted what you were offering."

"Sure, except . . . obviously not." She danced her fingers down his chest in a parody of their earlier contact—then quit when even that got her motor racing again. He caught her hand before she could successfully pull away.

"The only part that didn't was the tiny bit that sensed what you were selling was a lie."

"What I was *selling*?" She tried to yank her hand free, but he held fast.

"A quickie won't get me out of your system, Samantha—or vice versa."

A slow sizzle of heat moved from the pressure of his hand on hers all the way up her arm—and then beyond, far beyond. "Oh, yeah?"

"Yeah."

He took her cup with his free hand, placed it on the table beside his, then rested his hand on her bare knee. His skin was warm against her flesh and made her shiver.

"Well, I didn't say it had to be quick," she said, fighting for a semblance of control.

He dragged his thumb along her bottom lip and she caught it with her teeth. Her stomach tightened with delicious anticipation when his breath hitched. "Before we start anything I want you to know that Maureen was my first, and believe it or not, I haven't been with anyone since."

Sam almost yelped in disbelief. "What?" All the syrupy sweet heat spreading through her froze and turned brittle. She got to her feet. "No, I'm sorry—but you were right last light. Whatever this is, you, me . . . " She shook her head. "It shouldn't be happening."

Charlie's eyes widened, but then he smiled cautiously. "Don't worry. I'm not totally inept. You won't be disappointed."

Sam waved a hand. "I don't care about that—or I do, but sex is kinda like pizza. Even when it's bad, it's still pretty good."

"*What*?"

"It's not going to work, sorry."

His voice was stunned now. "So just like that you're on, and now you're totally off? Why? Because I'm not into a one night stand or because I'm not some big player?"

"Because you obviously take life very seriously—and good for you. It's a good thing, or at least not a bad thing . . . but it's not me. You're not the kind of guy I want."

Charlie had joined her standing and was so close

Sam could feel his breath on her face, slightly minty still despite his coffee. He took a stride back and pondered her words. "I don't know what to say to that."

Sam cupped Charlie's face with her palms. "I know, Charlie. Case in point."

His shoulders sagged and for a split second she entertained a fantasy: what if neither of them were who they were today, without the pasts they each had, what then? Would he or someone like him be her type after all? But then the grating noise of metal on ice and a growl of heavy machinery in the parking area brought her to her senses.

"If it's any consolation," she added on the way to her room, "this is much easier, less messy, for both of us."

"And that's always the top priority, right? Whatever's easiest and the least messy?"

She turned back, surprised at his sharp tone. "Well, of course. What else would be?"

Chapter 18

SAMANTHA OPENED THE DOOR AND Charlie barreled past her. He was acting like kenneled dog freed at last, but he didn't care. The cabin was suddenly claustrophobic. What had just happened? Was he really just turned down because he didn't want completely casual sex? And what was he? A complete idiot? What guy who'd been celibate as long as he had said no to a bit of no-strings-attached fun?

The cold air was a truth serum straight from his lungs to his heart. Him, that's who. *He* was that guy. Dammit, Samantha had totally pegged him. So what was it that he found so attractive about her? That she was the opposite of him—and of Maureen—in every way? Or that he sensed deep down she, for all her bravado, was actually as scared of closeness as he was?

The grater rumbled over to the other side of the lot, spewing sand and gravel, but Charlie didn't get to enjoy the quiet for long. A black Hummer with lots of chrome and bumblebee yellow decals advertising some sort of fitness club took the driveway too fast. Chunks of salt and grit peppered Charlie's shirt and face.

"Slow down, asshole," he muttered as a huge blond guy climbed out of the driver's side.

"Sorry about that, dude," the man replied, obviously not sorry a bit.

Charles took in the stranger's tanned glow and gelled hair. What an idiot. He swallowed his irritation and stalked toward the main house. Some battles were worth fighting. Some weren't.

"Hey, fella. Wait up. This is Jo and Callum Archer's place, right?"

Charlie stopped. "Yeah," he said reluctantly.

"River's Sigh B & B—like the bed-and-breakfast?"

"*Yeah*." What kind of moron felt the need to clarify that "B & B" stood for bed-and-breakfast anyway?

"And that's the main house, like where Jo lives?"

Muscle-bound Guy nodded in the direction Charlie had been headed, but Charlie was slow to confirm it. He was getting a strange vibe. "Did you need something specific?" he asked, as if he had any right to get territorial about the place.

The guy took a step back, confirming Charlie's suspicion that something was up, and turned his head to scan the scattered cabins. "I'm looking for Sam."

Charlie started. Whatever he'd been expecting, it wasn't that. But then again, why wasn't it that? A woman like Samantha must have them lining up. What had he thought? That she was here just to torture him and be the focus of all his lame fantasies?

Charlie shook his head and the guy misread it. "She's not? Well, could you point me to which cabin is hers?"

The cobalt blue door on the main house banged opened, saving Charlie from having to answer.

"I thought I heard a vehicle pull up, hello—" The cheery greeting died on Jo's lips, and when she spoke again, Charlie was shocked by the change in her demeanor. Her voice was cold and her mouth twisted with contempt. "*Dave*. I'd say it was a pleasure, but you know better."

"Jo." The man raised his hand in greeting as if she hadn't just slammed him. "I'm here for Sam. She around?"

"You're here for Sam?" Jo's tone could've frozen salt water.

The "Dave" guy—whoever he was to everyone, obviously *someone*—shrugged amiably. Charlie walked over to stand closer to Jo.

"We're supposed to be getting together. I wanted to set up a time."

"You're supposed to be . . ." Jo echoed again, then trailed off. "Well, isn't that just bloody-fricken-typical," Jo said under her breath. She raised her eyebrows at Charles. "Well, *is* she there?"

He was saved from having to figure out what to say. Samantha's flirtatious laugh floated over to them. "Dave? Whatever brings you here?"

His grin was slow and practiced. "Would you believe me if I said I was in the neighborhood?"

Of all the oily, flashy creeps. For a heartbeat, Charlie thought he glimpsed contempt in Sam's face too, but then her laugh tinkled again.

"No," she said, her voice light and flirty. "I would not. What gives?"

"I've enjoyed seeing you at the gym, but what I'd really like to do is . . . well, let's start with dinner or something, shall we?"

Jo practically bared her teeth. Then she huffed and disappeared back into the house without another word.

Dave gave Charlie a grin. "Women, hey?"

Charlie assumed a stony expression, intentionally ignoring the comment; yet again Dave didn't acknowledge the snub. He just happily ambled over to Rainbow's deck and commenced chatting up Sam.

Burning off energy with a walk in the woods no longer seemed like it would be peaceful or productive—and why should he have to clear out of the cabin? It had been his first. He stomped over to where Samantha and Dave stood visiting and tried to brush past her and into the house.

Samantha touched Charlie's forearm. "Have you met Dave?" she asked.

"Yeah, I've met him all right." He continued forward without pause.

She didn't follow him inside.

He skulked around, putting on water for tea, setting

up a lamp for better light to work by, digging up a snack—all the time knowing what he was really doing: listening for her return. The kettle had just whistled when the Hummer started outside the window and roared away, followed by Sam in her SUV. He sighed. Obviously his other guesses had been off track. The reason Samantha declined his advance once she was sober is that she had some other guy on the line. Thank God they hadn't gotten together when they were drunk. He didn't need that kind of heartbreak.

He looked at the clock. Visiting hours started soon. A happy lightness coursed through him, dispelling his gloom. He had a granddaughter!

He went through the motions of planning out a writing schedule that he'd keep for the remainder of his time at River's Sigh, so he'd be able to get a rough draft done in time and left the isolated cabin.

At the hospital, he could barely refrain from running to the elevator and down the hall to Aisha's room.

"Dad," she exclaimed as he practically peeled out turning into her doorway. "Great news! We're cleared to go home tomorrow morning."

"You're not kidding? That's fantastic! What changed your mind?"

In the dead silence that followed his overly enthusiastic response, Charlie realized two things. One—by "home," Aisha had meant her cabin at River's Sigh. Two—Samantha had beaten him to the hospital and was sitting by the window, staring at him just as incredulously as Aisha was. *Shit.*

"I'm sorry. I'm an idiot. You meant your cabin—still great news. Where's Mo?"

Aisha pointed to a swath of white flannel decorated with tiny yellow ducks, resting between her legs on top of the blue hospital linens.

"No way," Charlie said, momentarily forgetting his conflicted feelings about running into Sam so soon—Sam who *hadn't* gone off with Dave after all. "She can't be wrapped in that. It's too tiny."

Aisha lifted the bundle, the soft fabric shifted and Charlie did indeed catch a glimpse of a little pink face. Mo squirmed and made a mewling grunting noise.

"Poor little tyke," Sam said. "I hate getting disturbed while I'm sleeping too."

"I'll take that under advisement," Charlie said, only catching the implications of his comment when Sam's soft, throaty laugh sounded.

"Gross, Dad," Aisha added, but there wasn't any heat in her words. Apparently she'd decided he and Sam weren't really at risk of getting together, or else she was just too preoccupied with postpartum delight over Mo. Either way. Good.

Aisha shot a glance at Sam that he couldn't interpret, but then Mo turned her face toward his chest and nuzzled him, captivating them all once more.

"She's hungry," Aisha said. "She's caught onto nursing really quick."

She might as well have said Mo had already

learned to read or climbed Mount Everest, her voice was that proud—and Charlie's chest swelled too.

"Yep, she's a smartie all right."

Samantha's chair creaked and she got to her feet. "I should go," she said, approaching Aisha's bed. "I'll come by your cabin tomorrow on my way out."

She moved to Charlie's side next and stroked Mo's impossibly tiny hand. "Good-bye little one," she whispered. Mo's fingers starfished at Sam's touch, then wrapped around Sam's index finger. "Oh," she said. "Look at that."

"She doesn't want you to go," Aisha said. "And neither do I. Dad, Sam was saying it wasn't really working for her to stay with you, and—"

"What? I never said that."

"No, no, he truly didn't. He's been very generous, but that doesn't change the fact. I'm in his way," Sam interrupted quickly.

"Is she, Dad? Really?"

"Well, no. . . ." But also yes, totally. Charlie studied Mo's tiny crescent moon fingernails and her possessive grip on Sam's pretty, French-tipped finger. And he looked at his daughter's expectant face. How selfish was he? Of course he could put up with some temporary discomfort. If Aisha wanted Sam in her life, he wouldn't be the one to come between them.

"I'm sorry if I was rude or made you feel unwelcome. I've just been . . ." His voice trailed off. What could he say, after all? I've just been going out of my mind with desire for you? I can hardly think when you're around. I want you to see me as relationship material, not just a quick screw? I don't want you to like that jerk Dave. Maybe he should just be bold and say all those things. Put them out there. Why not? His heart pounded even thinking of it.

"Earth to Dad. *Dad*." Aisha's laugh pulled him out of his head. "He's in the middle of a book. It makes him even more spacey than usual."

Sam's smile was a bit wicked. "Is that so, Charlie? Your writing has you all crazy right now? Poor guy."

Aisha's eyes narrowed and her gaze swung from his face to Sam's and back to his again. So maybe she wasn't completely appeased after all. But he couldn't bring himself to obsess about what Aisha might or might not be worrying about. His sole focus was on Sam. He was so aware of her nearness—and the fact that she knew full well it wasn't his novel making him distracted. Yet he latched onto the excuse anyway.

"What Aisha said." Charles nodded. "And ditto what she said about you not being in my way. If you can endure it, you're welcome to stay as long as you need—or want. It would mean a lot, actually."

Sam gave him a long, considering look. "Well, if you're sure . . . then, yes, I'd love to stay a few more days."

"Good, it's settled." For some reason, like an idiot, he stuck out his hand. Shaking her head, Sam grinned, slipped her hand into his, and shook firmly.

"Get some chapters done tonight," Aisha advised as Sam said good-bye once more and slipped from the room. Charlie's eyes followed her.

"What? Oh, yeah, yeah—I will. Made up a plan and everything, kiddo."

"Uh huh," said Aisha cryptically. "I bet you did."

Chapter 19

CHARLIE WAS STILL AT THE hospital and the parking area at River's Sigh was empty. Samantha stood on Rainbow's porch, keys in hand, but didn't unlock the door. Instead she turned this way and that, marveling at the greenery that flanked her on all sides in such bright and vivid contrast to the white blanket spread by the freak storm. Everything was so alive here, yet simultaneously quiet and still. It felt annoyingly catching. Since when was she calmed by solitude and fresh air? And speaking of fresh air—the incessant wind had finally let up and the air was warmer as Jo had promised. The gravel was shiny with water running in small rivers from the already melting snow heaps.

Just as she was about to go inside, she caught a trembling movement out of the corner of her eye. She turned and saw a glimpse of tan fur disappear under a cedar hedge. She crouched and peered into the bushes, but couldn't see a thing.

Jo's beat up old truck ambled into the parking lot, then bee-lined for Rainbow cabin when Sam waved.

"Oh, Sam, great," Jo called through the open driver's side window. "I was hoping I'd run into you. Do you want to go fishing?"

"Do I want to go *fishing*? I don't know—the thought's never occurred to me before."

"Oh, come on. If you're really leaving soon, you should see a bit of the property. I'll bring coffee."

"Well, I was going to . . . actually never mind. Sure, why not? Throw in some Kahlua too and I'm in."

"Done! I'll meet you back here in ten minutes—and I'll bring you appropriate footwear."

Sam groaned and they both laughed.

∼

SAM'S REFLECTION STARED UP AT her from the nearly black face of the smooth deep pool they'd been fishing in and she noted the moisture in the air had ruined her straightening job. Her hair was curling around her face a lot like Jo's actually—and she didn't even care that much. "That was really fun."

Jo laughed and handed Sam the tackle box they were finished with. "You don't have to sound so surprised. Maybe next time you'll even catch something."

"Gross. Let's not get carried away."

They headed back the way they'd come, tramping along a path that had knee-deep snow in some places and was mossy green and almost dry in other spots where the tree cover was especially thick.

Their conversation had run the gamut from what it was like meeting little Mo, to Jo's plans for the next cabins—and Jo's lack of surprise that Sam had some design ideas fueled by her recent magazine splurge—to how Jo found married life. It had been light and fun and now Sam was more than content to walk in silence. In fact, she would've preferred it. No such luck, though.

"So have you figured out what you're going to do next?"

Shit. Why had she blabbed about wanting a life change to Jo? Now Jo would expect updates.

"Not yet, but some ideas are finally stirring." Sam made the comment mainly to satisfy Jo, but realized it was sort of true. She paused by an archway created by two huge cedars that had grown up close together, separate and distinct but birthed from the same root system. She rested a hand on each rough trunk and leaned forward. The tree-window offered a spectacular view of a jutting rock face and rushing creek.

Jo pointed up the creek. "There's a gorgeous canyon beyond that bend. We could hike to it sometime if you're game."

"Is it a tough climb?"

"Not too bad, no. And there's a good trail."

They resumed walking and Sam thought that if a person could somehow bottle the smell of the air around here she might stop buying perfume. And she loved perfume.

"Sam . . ."

A note in Jo's voice made Sam feel slightly alarmed. "What?"

"Have you talked to Aisha about her dad yet?"

"I talk to her about Charlie quite a bit, yes."

"Come on."

Sam picked up her pace, passing Jo. The trail was wide and obvious. She didn't need Jo to lead her home. "No, but I've been ready to. She hasn't asked."

"She's worried it's a painful subject."

"It *is* a painful subject."

"Yeah." Jo closed the gap between them again, but stayed shoulder-to-shoulder with Sam, matching her stride. "But I think she thinks she might be the product of rape or something."

"Oh." Sam stopped moving abruptly. "*Oh.* Well, yeah, I guess I should clear that up."

When she got back to Rainbow and said good-bye to Jo, her mind was a jumble of contrasting thoughts and memories from both the far past and the near present. So much for nature clearing your head—but it was a good muddle, the kind that comes just before small epiphanies, so that was all right.

"Sam?" Charlie exited his bedroom and stood near where she was taking off the hiking boots Jo had lent her. "We should talk about some things."

"Agreed," she said, making her voice bright and light. "But can I beg a rain check? I need to do some work first."

"What? Oh, yeah, of course."

She darted a glance at the stove's clock in the kitchen. "Let's say a late dinner, eight-ish, maybe? That'll give us two hours to work. Half an hour to make food. I'll cook."

Charlie's smile resurfaced finally. "Sounds good," he said. "Sounds really good."

⤝

CHARLIE TYPED, OH DID HE ever—but he wasn't thinking about a word he wrote. Samantha had settled herself in one corner of the living room after starting a cheerful blaze in the fireplace.

"Will it disturb you if I work in the living room, too?" she'd asked.

Like the idiot he was when it came to her, he'd answered, "No, no, of course not." He didn't regret the lie though. Not one bit.

He kept sneaking looks at her, but she was so absorbed in whatever she was doing online that he was pretty sure she didn't notice. He wanted to ask her what she was working on, something to do with the ambiguous investing she'd referred to maybe? For some reason, he'd assumed she lived on some big divorce settlement or something or the inheritance she and Jo had—but now that he knew her a bit better, she actually didn't seem like the type to be dependent on someone else's generosity. Most of her entitlement and princess behavior seemed more like a game or her sense of humor than her legitimate personality.

Every so often she muttered something he couldn't quite catch in response to something on one of the many screens she was clicking through—and it hit him that he'd heard her on her laptop frequently, usually in the morning. He'd just assumed she was checking social media sites or reading news or something. Maybe she'd been working.

Man, he was curious. But he resisted asking. Just.

All of a sudden, her eyes shot up and caught his stare. His blood thrummed, warming his face, and he glanced away quickly.

He focused hard on his monitor then and managed to get into the story for a while—and then she shifted her position and he chanced another quick ogle. What on earth was so fascinating about her working on a computer nearby in quiet?

Actually, scratch that. He knew exactly what he was enjoying. The cozy feeling of companionship that came with shared quiet and industry. It was a lovely, comfortable thing to sit and work side by side with someone.

A rustling sound caught his attention again. Sam opened a foil-wrapped candy and popped it in her mouth, then closed her laptop and picked up a spiral bound notebook.

She wrote steadily without pause and Charlie found

his flow in her rhythm and the soft shhh of her hand moving across the page.

Eventually she stretched her lovely arms above her head and sighed. Charlie did the same. "Time's up already?"

"No, you still have fifteen minutes or so—actually, you could keep going until dinner's ready, if you want."

"You don't need help?"

She shook her head. "Nope. I'm good. Did you get anything done?"

"Yeah, yeah, of course. Why?"

"I don't know. For a little while there it was almost like I was *being watched*."

Her grin said she was joking, making light of earlier.

"Ha ha," he said, though what he wanted to do was hug her. Which was ridiculous.

"So what were you working on anyway?" she asked.

"Nothing. Just a scene in the story."

Sam's head tilted slightly. She seemed to be waiting for something—and then she laughed. "Oh, that's it, your full answer. I get it. Well, it sounds . . . very compelling."

Charlie laughed too. "Sorry. I didn't figure you wanted details."

"Well, I asked, didn't I? I only ask things I want to know or do things I want to do."

"Is that so?"

"That is so." She nodded her head with emphasis.

"Do you want to read what I have so far?" He couldn't believe he was asking, even as the words poured out. He never offered that. And he was even more alarmed when Sam stood up, looking delighted.

"Really?" she asked.

He winced. "I guess. If you actually want to."

"I'd love to—but aren't you starved?"

"No, I'm okay. I can wait."

"Great."

He handed her his laptop, knowing it had finally happened: he'd lost his mind.

"I'm not very far in and it's early stages and—"

"No disclaimers needed."

"It won't take you long."

"What if I'm a really slow reader?"

"Well, yes, I guess, but even then—"

"I'm joking. I'm joking, and hey, if you've changed your mind or don't feel comfortable. . . ."

"No, no. Go ahead. I'd like to hear what you think actually." It horrified him to realize that was true.

She shrugged. "Great, but don't expect any deep comments. I love to read, but I don't know anything about stories. Numbers are more my thing."

He handed off his laptop and headed to his room, planning to grab a shower before dinner. He liked watching her work, sure, but it would be agony observing her read his work. He'd drive himself crazy trying to decipher whether or not she was enjoying it at all.

He shaved, showered, and threw on jeans and a clean T-shirt. Then he read two chapters in a paperback he'd grabbed at the hospital gift shop. Finally he got to his feet and paced his small bedroom. It was taking too long. She'd hated it, absolutely hated it, and didn't know how to tell him.

He couldn't bear it another second. He trucked out to the living room in bare feet.

She was motionless on the couch, staring down at his laptop as if in a trance. She literally jumped when she noticed him. "I . . . I really have no idea what to say."

He held up a hand. "It's okay. You don't have to say anything. First drafts are always terrible. It'll change a lot—"

"No." She shook her head. "I loved it. I was . . . surprised how much, actually."

"Surprised how? Why?"

"It's feels very real and sweet. They're both so broken in different ways. I want them to fix themselves—or maybe not, maybe just somehow find happiness together as they are."

"Really? You're not just being nice? You're truly rooting for them?"

She nodded and lifted the laptop up to him. "Absolutely. And Gil is totally hot. I love him."

Charlie wanted to ask a hundred questions, but Sam was shaking her head and adding something else.

"Only one thing with Simone. Don't overdo the whole cold bitch thing is merely a cover up for a mushy heart. I'll buy it to a point but the two qualities aren't mutually exclusive. Don't make her toughness a flaw. And also, now I'm just being silly though, don't make her a brunette. I want her to be a blonde like me." She laughed. "I know. Ego much?"

Charlie blanched, but Sam had already turned away. Surely she couldn't have recognized herself in Simone? No, that would be beyond mortifying.

"But enough. You shouldn't care what I think anyway. Like you said, the book will change a bunch before you're through—and now I am making dinner because I'm starving."

He nodded to her retreating figure. "And you're sure you don't need help?"

"I'm sure—actually wait. I have one more book-related question." She turned back to him. "The couple of times things started to get steamy, you put triangle brackets around the word 'action.' Is that your weird writer slang for sex? Everything's so fluid to that point. . . . Do you freeze up or something?"

He'd totally forgotten about those notes to himself. "Uh, well, there are only two—"

"So? I wanted to know what happened."

Charlie's whole body warmed. It was like he was in a state of constant embarrassment around her—and a constant state of something else too, come to think of it.

She was looking at him expectantly. What the heck, he thought. I let her read a first draft. I might as well go for full humiliation. "I don't freeze up writing sex scenes, no. The opposite actually. I really enjoy them."

Sam's pupils dilated slightly—or maybe that was just his overactive imagination again. "Oh, you do, do you?"

"I do." He cleared his throat. "But I have this thing I like to do, sort of a practice thing, to see if something I'm visualizing would work in real life and be remotely sexy or plausible or whatever."

"Well, well, well," Sam said. "You naughty boy. And just who, for the sake of literary integrity, do you practice these moves on?" She froze. "Oh, no—wait. Your wife, right? That's what you meant when you said you told her stories. I'm so sorry."

Charlie shook his head. "Don't apologize. Maureen, yes—but it was a long while ago now. It's probably why I haven't written anything new in years."

Sam looked down and Charlie could've kicked himself. Instead, to his shock, he reached out and touched her cheek. "I could show you."

Her gaze slid up to meet his again, and the corners of her mouth lifted. "Oh, *really*? And just what do you mean by that?"

"Well, the book's in early days. . . . You don't have to worry about being completely ravished or anything."

"I don't have to worry about—" Sam echoed, then broke out laughing. The sound faded and was replaced by a contemplative look and a raised brow. "Okay, writer man. Put your moves where your words are." She giggled again.

Charlie's eyes held hers until she quieted and bit her lip, returning his study. He took her hand and smoothed a slow, constant circle over the base of her palm with his thumb.

"Here's the thing, Sam," he said in a low voice, quoting Gil, but using her name instead of Simone's. "I know you find me attractive—and you can keep fighting it. Or you can give into it and have some fun."

Sam hesitated and her eyes narrowed—but then she spoke, her voice wobbling with a small tremor of fury tinged with unmistakable desire. "Of all the arrogant, presumptuous, idiotic—"

Charlie was a little taken aback. She was really good at this already.

He increased the pressure of his touch on her hand. "So say it then. Say you don't want me."

"I. Don't. Want. You."

Charlie snugged his arm around her waist and pulled her close. "Then this won't have any effect." He bent his head to her neck, kissed just below her ear, midway down her throat, just above her clavicle. . . .

"None whatsoever," she said, but her back arched slightly, belying her words.

"I don't believe you."

"Then you're an idiot."

"And what if I do this?" Charlie kissed along her collarbone, then flicked the mesmerizing hollow of her throat lightly with his tongue.

Sam went rigid against him. "Holy shit, Charlie. I—"

"I thought you didn't want me," he growled.

"I don't. I can't. . . ."

"Don't or can't or *won't*?" he whispered.

"This is a very bad idea."

"Or a really, really good one."

"No—"

He leaned back and licked his lips, then smiled at how her gaze followed the movement. "I'll tell you what. I'll make you a deal."

"What kind of a deal?" Her voice was breathy and rough. Charlie swallowed hard and traced his finger from her mouth, along the line of her jaw, then down the curve of her body until he reached her hip. "You give me five minutes of freedom and don't make a noise of passion or response, and I'll take your word at face value and back off."

"And . . . if I do make a noise?"

"Well, then all deals are off."

She stepped back and planted her feet, almost in a fighting stance. "You flatter yourself—and your abilities."

Charlie wanted to laugh out loud. She'd ad-libbed, changing the line Simone had used, and it was a good change, one he'd steal with her permission. He laced his hands behind her head, but stayed his full arms' length away from her.

"Aren't you going to start a timer or something?" she demanded in an irritated tone.

He shook his head and gave her a slow, cocky smile. "I won't need a timer. I'll have you purring in a hot minute."

Sam almost cracked a grin, then managed to shove it away. Something tugged deep and low in Charlie's gut, and he hoped like hell he could pull this off. It wasn't like any other time. He'd have to put the brakes on; the thought was nipped off by Sam's saucy look.

He started slowly, kneading the back of her head—and smiled as she put a foot forward and settled her weight. It was a tell whether she knew it or not, a way of trying to avoid her body's desire to loll against his in a natural response to pleasure. He moved lower, working his hands through the tension in the muscles at the base of her neck and between her shoulder blades.

"You're so tight," he whispered, then realizing what it sounded like he could be saying, he played the line harder. "You should let me loosen you up."

Sam snorted. "We've already established you want me, tight or not," she whispered back, still sounding all too cool for Charlie's liking.

He slid his hands down her sides, found the waistband of her jeans and slipped his hands up the back of her soft knit shirt, exposing an inch or two of skin.

She shivered—and a fraction of a second later said, "Brr. Cold."

"Good cover," Charlie said, then tugged her against him and tilted her chin up to face him. She stared at him defiantly.

"That's right. Keep your eyes open. I want to watch you respond to me." It was probably harder for him than her to maintain control as he closed the distance between their faces, touched his lips to hers, then opened her mouth with his tongue—but somehow he managed.

Her mouth tasted like the cinnamon candy she'd been sucking earlier and was everything he'd imagined and more. He was losing himself in their kiss. . . .

Head in the game, man, head in the game, he lectured. He felt her start to kiss back and pulled away slightly, spread his legs, and pulled her closer still.

"Oh my—" she breathed against his mouth.

"What was that?" he prompted.

She stubbornly bit her lip, said nothing.

"That's right," he affirmed. "The longer you can manage to stay quiet, the more we can play."

She glared. He smiled. And moved his hands from where they'd rested under the lower edge of her shirt up the silky expanse of her back. He was hard as a rock and shifted a bit, letting her get the full effect—

Her mouth fell open under his this time, with no pressure from his tongue and he held her head while he kissed her, then moved back to her neck and traveled down it.

"Just admit you want me as much as I want you," he said against her skin.

"But I don't."

He let go of her suddenly and she sagged against him. He steadied her and pulled her to himself again, hard. "Well, I want you," he said, kissing her shoulder. "You make me crazy—and all I want is a chance to make you as crazy as you make me. I want your breasts in my mouth—"

Sam shuddered. He massaged her silky lower back in widening circles, then eased his hands down to her buttocks. He pressed his lips to hers once more, then whispered against her mouth, "and I want to make you scream my name." As he spoke, he cupped her ass and squeezed.

"Ohh—" The guttural sound came from deep in Sam's throat, a heat-filled groan of desire intertwined with surprise. Charlie had to pull in a long breath to steady himself against his own response to the noise.

He forced himself to pull back, but kept his hands lightly on Sam's forearms. "I win," he purred—then hoped his voice was steady as he narrated in a formal tone, "But Gil's gloating was cut short. A door slammed open and sharp, staccato footsteps approached. An angry, all too familiar voice shrilled, 'Are you kidding me?'—Insert chapter break."

Sam stepped back too, her breathing ragged. "To

heck with Simone. You'll have everyone screaming."

Charlie shrugged and couldn't quite hold back his satisfied smile.

Her eyes locked with his and her chin lifted. Finally she spoke again, shaking her head a little. "Well, well, well, Writer-guy. You're full of surprises, aren't you?"

"What can I say? I'm studious and read a lot."

"Read, my ass. You didn't learn that in a book."

Charlie grinned. Of course he had. Where else would he have learned anything? "Well, you know, a gentleman never tells."

"I'm no longer convinced you are a gentleman."

"Oh, touché—that really hurts."

Sam smirked. "But seriously, will the scene end like that?"

"End with Simone grunting with wanton desire against her will? Absolutely."

Sam smacked him. "No, will they get interrupted or will they continue on, you know, to the end."

"Unbearably disappointed, were you?"

"No, yeah—shut up." Sam returned his grin. "I just want to know."

Charlie hesitated. The last time he'd tried to explain his take on sexuality, she hadn't been impressed. He didn't want to offend her again. But he couldn't pretend he was legitimately like Gil, either—or not on all counts anyway.

"Yeah, that's where the scene will end. I'm a takes-sex-seriously guy and most of my characters are too. There's lots of fun and games, but they don't hook up until they know there's something real between them."

Sam chewed the edge of one knuckle, something Charlie had never seen her do, then noticed what she was doing and moved her hand to rest on her hip. "So you're a hardcore happily ever guy, hey?"

"I used to be anyway." A touch of melancholy threatened his newfound cheer, but he maintained eye contact with Sam. "And I'm starting to hope I will be again one day."

Sam looked away. "Well, I'm more of an H.F.N.— or better yet, an S.B.S.G.B." *Happily for now*, I get, but what's the other one?"

A sardonic smile twisted Sam's mouth. "Stop before shit gets bad."

"Well, if it's any consolation, you're probably the smarter of us."

A flash of what looked like disappointment darkened Sam's eyes, but before he could ask her why, she laughed and he figured he was imagining things.

"We should eat. I'm starved," she announced. "Give me ten minutes."

Good to her word, a steamy aroma that Charlie couldn't quite place soon filled the small cabin.

"Come and get it," Sam called.

He obediently—and very happily—settled at the table. Sam produced a plate of sliced cheddar, a dish of saltines, a sandwich baggie of carrot and celery sticks, and two bowls of—

"Canned vegetable soup?" Charlie asked.

"In all its glory. R—reduced sodium too, in case you care."

Charlie started laughing.

"What?" Sam asked in a mildly affronted tone. "Carbs, protein, veggies . . . It's not great, but it's not the worst."

Charlie laughed harder.

"I told you I don't cook."

He couldn't stop laughing.

"I don't get it. What's so funny?" But Sam's voice held a trace of giggles too.

"I . . . I just . . . " Charlie wheezed. "Never in a million years took you as a canned soup girl. I always thought you were joking."

"Shows what you know. Whenever, *if* ever, I turn on the stove, canned soup's involved."

"I would have predicted, I don't know, roasted squash, goat cheese and arugula pizza, or bruschetta and—"

"Pizza crust and crispy bread? Too many carbs, no thanks. And as for those other things . . . I like food well enough, but I'm not having a bloody affair with it like Jo is. Who has the time? Enjoy the crackers and say thanks for dinner."

"Thank you for dinner," Charlie said softly. "It's perfect."

Sam made a face and crunched a piece of celery,

loudly.

"I'm serious. I love it."

"You're easy to please."

"No, I'm not."

They ate for a few minutes in silence and Charlie really did feel it was one of the best meals he'd enjoyed in a long time. Sam had shared her real self with him, not a meant-to-impress version.

"I had a really nice time today," Sam said eventually. "And I don't just mean the, uh, playacting."

Immediately all Charlie could think of was how Sam felt in his arms, how her mouth . . . and it wasn't helpful. "I enjoyed myself too."

"Thanks for letting me stay here."

"The pleasure really is mine."

Sam put her spoon down. "So are we going to be all stilted and awkward from here on out?"

"No . . . no. It's just weird, you know?"

"Yes, I do."

The rest of their meal rapidly disappeared. "I really like you, Charlie."

"And I like you."

Sam rolled her eyes. "This is ridiculous."

"Yes—"

She held up her hand to stop whatever he was about to say. "And I'm flattered that you like me. Not a lot of men do."

"There's no way that's true."

Sam shrugged. "Okay, fine, but there are very few

men—very few people, actually—that I like."

That Charlie did believe, but only because she made her walls so high. If she let her guard down for an instant . . .

As they ate, just like whenever they were together it seemed, they chatted easily and non-stop, even covering weird things like where they'd gone to school and what they'd wanted to be when they grew up.

"Astronaut," Charlie said. "But the closest I got was a character who dated someone who worked at NASA."

Sam laughed wryly. "An actress—and in some ways that's exactly what I became." Her mouth clamped shut then, like she was slightly shocked, maybe annoyed, by the admission.

Charlie nodded. He didn't have to ask what she meant by that. He knew. Just like she knew she'd taken down part of her carefully constructed wall.

A moment later, she yawned and stretched. "Man, I'm beat."

"I'll do the dishes."

"Are you sure?"

"Absolutely. I won't be able to sleep for a while anyway."

"Well, I'm never going to do dishes voluntarily, so I accept your offer." She rolled her napkin and touched it lightly to his shoulder like she was knighting him.

"Do you want a glass of wine or anything before you go off to bed?"

Sam rolled her neck, and then looked at him from under heavy lids. "More than anything but I'm passing. Thanks."

She stood up, but instead of moving down the hallway, she paused beside him. "I just want one last kiss," she said softly. "You and me though, not Gil and Simone."

He was touched and didn't bother to mention that he was Gil *and* Simone and pretty much all and every one of his characters, no matter how villainous, sweet, sane or screwed up.

She bent down and her warm, soft lips settled on his mouth, and her tongue gently teased his—and then she stopped and straightened. "And just so you know," she whispered.

"Yeah?"

"Your hero who's lost his wife and his way, who wants a wild affair but realizes it's just not him. . . ."

Charlie's heart pounded. What she must think of him, a sad, pitiful—

Sam continued softly. "He's worried Simone thinks he's pathetic, but she doesn't. Not at all. She's scared of him. Someone that principled and hopeful is hard to measure up around."

Her green eyes weren't just hard to read now; they were impossible. She pressed her hand to his cheek for just a second. It was cool and smooth against his flesh that suddenly felt like it might spontaneously combust.

"Good night, Charlie. Sleep well."

"Good night," he managed to choke out. The kiss, so sweet, was seared into his mind along with her words. He couldn't explain exactly how he knew, but he did. Samantha Kendall, the furthest thing from the arch nemesis he'd imagined, the biological mother of his child, his granddaughter's grandma, and more and more, someone he couldn't bear not having in his life, had just said good-bye.

Her next words confirmed it. "You referred to the fun and games in your stories earlier—and that's what we've been doing, playing games. I initiate, you back off—you initiate, I back off, etc., etc. And it's been fun, but it won't stay that way. You know we can't keep it up."

He shrugged, feeling about twelve-years-old: angry and rebellious about what she was saying, but pretty sure she was right.

"I don't know if I want to be part of Aisha and Mo's life—or if I even can be really—but I definitely don't want to have an affair with you that ends badly, or risks burning any bridges that may or may not exist between us. I'm sorry I toyed with you."

Toyed with him. Was that all their chats and contact had been to her, really? Didn't even a small bit of their fledgling relationship feel like something that needed more exploration? "Why would it have to end badly? Why couldn't it work? It could work."

Sam shook her head. "You don't really mean that. I'm just the first person to stir your interest since you've started to emerge from the darkest parts of your grief. You'll come to your senses. We're not a good match."

"Stop telling me what I supposedly 'know' and what I 'really' mean."

"Oh, Charlie, let's be real. You're a food and family kind of person. You eat up small town life. I've overheard you talking to Jo and listened while you visit Aisha. You adore everything I hate. Making soup is extravagant cooking on my part; half the time I prefer to drink my dinner. I like to go out, spend wildly, take vacations on a whim. I don't want to be tied down by family or relationships or commitments."

Charlie studied Sam's smooth, pretty face. Then he nodded very slowly. "Well, if you're sure of that, I guess you're right. But I have to ask . . . if all that's true, why are you here with me and Aisha and Mo now? Why do you keep saying you're taking off, then changing your mind? And even before we were in the picture, why were you in Greenridge for almost a year with Jo? There was nothing about the handling of your uncle's estate that couldn't have been done from a distance. And you never go out. You're as much as a homebody as me. You're not the only one who listens, who watches."

Sam started to reply, but Charlie interrupted. "Just think about it. Maybe I'm out to lunch, or maybe you're more like me than you want to admit. Ready for a change and to let something—someone—new into your life after too many years of shutting doors to keep pain at bay."

"You write too many romances, Chuck. And as I admitted, they're lovely—but they're also *fiction*. Real life isn't like that."

Charlie wanted to say she was wrong, that of course true love was real, could be healing, did overcome crazy obstacles. He turned toward the kitchen to start on the dishes. "Just think about it," he repeated. "That's all I'm asking."

His thoughts weren't on Sam when she left though. They were on himself. And Maureen. *I want to believe again,* he thought to her, *so maybe you were right. Maybe love is worth any potential pain.*

Standing there, alone in the empty kitchen, shoulders hunched and wrists submerged in graying, soapy water, his whole body shook. Not with sorrow. Not with relief. With gratitude. Regardless of what, if anything, became of him and Sam, perhaps there was an end to the dark tunnel he'd been trapped in, a clear exit to which small lights had been leading him all along. He just hadn't been able to see it until now.

Chapter 20

THE SPEEDY CLICK-CLICK-CLICK OF FINGERS on a keyboard was louder in the hallway, but Sam had been able to hear it in her room too. Charlie was madly working away and had been since at least 4:00 a.m.

She decided not to disturb his flow just to tell him she was heading out for a while. He'd learn of her new accommodations soon enough.

She moved all her things to the porch, then quietly latched the door shut behind her. The outside air was damp and chilly, but also sweet with an invigorating hint of warmer days to come. It took her three trips and four curse words—one of which was caused by a soaker from a deep puddle—to move her stuff across the parking area and back into Silver cabin.

Returning from her last trip, she again considered popping into Rainbow to let Charlie know Jo had texted her to say Silver was available, but she'd no doubt see him later that afternoon when Aisha and Mo returned. Besides, Callum was already waiting for her by the SUV, hands shoved deep in his pockets.

"I hope this is no trouble," Callum said, scowling.

Sam took a step back. "None at all." She hit the unlock button on her key fob. "I was already up. Are you okay?"

Callum sighed heavily and pushed a hand through his hair. "I'm fine, perfectly fine."

"Yeah, *that's* convincing. Don't tell me there's trouble in paradise. Is Jo all right?"

Just hearing Jo's name seemed to bring him out of his funk a little. "Sorry, Sam. Yes, Jo's great as ever. There's just a bunch of family drama as usual and I get tired of it. My mom, Caren—have you met her?"

Sam had met her, just once, a long time ago, but she shook her head.

"She's thinking about leaving my dad, way past time if you ask me. My dad's brilliant response? He wants to throw a thirty-fifth wedding anniversary combo family reunion thing this fall. Here at River's Sigh. It's insane—and now my car's out of commission and I'm inconveniencing you—"

Sam pushed him lightly toward the vehicle. "I told you it's no problem. Just go. This place isn't so lame that being trapped here all day will kill me."

That did it. Callum finally smiled, shaking his head. "Jo should be back around lunchtime or shortly thereafter, so you could always drive her pickup if you—"

"I'd never be that desperate." She handed him her keys.

"I was just saying, *in case*. And the shop promises my car should be fixed by tomorrow, so I just need to put you out for the one day."

"Would you leave already? Please. I'll be great. I've already moved all my bags back to Silver and I have enough groceries to tide me over. . . . I'm going to go for a short walk, have the longest bath imaginable, then read and watch TV all day and not talk to another soul—well, I might pop by to see Aisha. Then again, I might just let her get settled and visit her tomorrow instead."

"Sounds nice." Callum got into the vehicle and started it.

Sam tapped on driver side window just as he put into gear.

He unrolled it a little.

"Try not to worry too much about your family stuff. I know crazy well. It'll work itself out—or it won't—but either way, stewing about it won't help."

He considered her words, and nodded. "Thanks, Sam. Really."

As the Mercedes purred down the driveway, Sam adjusted her shoulder bag's strap and felt around inside it to confirm she'd remembered her journal and breakfast—an insulated mug of coffee, bag of beef jerky, and small container of almonds—then tucked her cell phone into the bag's side pocket. She wanted to check out that pretty place by the rocks she'd spotted with Jo. If it wasn't too freezing, she'd do some writing there. Charlie's last comments to her were still chaffing. Yes, she'd been feeling a need to get her life sorted and to pick a new direction . . . but surely she wasn't pining away for what he seemed to be suggesting? At first it had shocked her, but as she lay awake late into the night she'd grudgingly admitted she liked being around Jo, Callum, Aisha, the baby, and Charlie more than she'd ever confess to anyone else. It scared the shit out of her, actually.

She took a deep breath and headed toward the trail she and Jo had taken together, hoping she could remember the right twists and turns—but worst-case scenario, even if she didn't, she had her phone.

A good half hour or so in, a snuffling-panting sound from deep in the greenery made her jump. Then she heard a small crash and the cracking of tiny twigs. When she saw a flash of fur, she laughed in relief. "Hoover, you idiot. Go home. Go home!"

There was no response or obvious compliance—but the mutt didn't even listen to Jo reliably so Sam wasn't surprised.

Before too long she was completely absorbed in the sound of her own breathing and her footfalls on the rapidly thawing earth. The terrain had changed even in the few days since she and Jo had gone fishing. It was a lot wetter, for one. So she wasn't delusional. Spring was on its way sooner rather than later.

When she came to the fork in the path she recognized as the one her and Jo had taken, she veered right and picked up her pace. Sure enough, she found an obvious trail that looked like it led the way through some craggy boulders in the right direction.

The river snaked, emerald and glistening, surprisingly far beneath her. She hadn't realized how much the path climbed as she walked. She turned a corner and her breath caught at the view. Looking straight down, it was clear she was at the mouth of the canyon Jo had mentioned. For a drop of easily one hundred feet or more, sheer-faced stone formed what looked exactly like the walls of some ancient castle that disappeared into a deep jade pool.

Just ahead, where the path switched directions and began a downward spiral, a massive tree hung out over the water, securely rooted in the mountain she stood on. Years of weather had broken off many of its branches, creating a natural bench. It was the perfect place for coffee and thoughts.

She sped up, grabbing her phone from her bag to take a picture as she did, completely focused on her destination rather than her next step—

A sickening sense of falling jerked in her stomach. She reached out to grab something, anything, but there was nothing. She dropped through empty air.

Sam hit a rocky ledge, tailbone first. Then her head bounced against something hard. Her left leg cracked itself over a jutting root like she was intentionally trying to damage herself. A roaring fire of pain blazed through her.

She half lay, half sat until her mind steadied—and then panicked again as she thought of her phone, her damn phone. She'd been holding it—and, of course, wasn't now. She glanced around frantically and caught a glimmer of bright metallic pink a few feet down from her on an impossibly narrow ledge. Her phone all right. But it might as well have fallen all the way to the bottom of the canyon for all the good it would do her there.

Sam tentatively pressed her fingers against her ankle and along her lower leg, hoping to determine how badly she was injured. She stopped almost immediately. The raging pain at even the gentlest touch made her think she'd vomit. She took a deep, steadying breath, peered down the sheer drop to the smooth as glass jade water, and shivered at how she'd only seen its beauty, not its danger. If she fell it would be like hitting concrete and she wasn't the best of swimmers in a heated pool, let alone waters just above freezing. Still . . . there was no need to panic. There were hours of daylight left and Callum knew she'd gone for a walk—wait, she had told him, right? Well, regardless, someone would notice she was gone. Or maybe the agony in her leg would subside. Maybe it was just a bad bruise. Maybe she would somehow be able to climb back up to the path and walk out.

Chapter 21

AGAINST HER WILL, SAM DRIFTED off. When she awoke
her head was pounding, her mental processes sluggish.
Damn, damn, damn, she thought. If I have a concus-
sion, it'll be the last straw. A minute or two passed and
she decided, no, her brain was fine. She was cold
though, and the pain in her leg and tailbone still raged.
She stretched a little, decided it was ridiculously unfair
that topping off everything else, the awkward position
she'd slept in had cricked her neck, and pondered the
sky. It was cloudy, something that was one part good,
one part bad, and one part worse. Good because it kept
the temperature relatively moderate. Bad and worse: It
made it hard to tell what time of day it was or how
much time had passed, and could potentially mean rain
or snow, which would be catastrophic for her.

Her focus dropped to her phone again. The case
shone tauntingly, snugly tucked against the cliff wall
by a small piney sprig. It was completely maddening.
The solution to her situation, perhaps even to her literal
survival, lay in plain sight but unquestionably out of

her reach. Damn it anyway!

She shifted her weight slightly, craning her head to look up. A fire bolt of pain shot through her at the minuscule movement, making her gasp. She estimated she was only eight or ten feet from the path, and a closer look revealed that the rocky face that appeared so smooth when gazing at it as a whole was actually marked by several uneven ledges like the one that caught her phone. They didn't seem as far apart as the one holding her phone hostage either. Could she climb them?

No. She shook her head and something Jo had mumbled at her sometime or another in one of her endless enthusiastic rants about nature was how if you ever did get lost you should stay put. Wait for a search party to find you. Too often people tried to find their way out of the woods and only ended up getting more lost, or falling and getting injured. And the award for managing all three of those things in one shot goes to? Sam laughed a little and the rasping sound startled her ears. And then suddenly there was another noise—but not a human one like she hoped for.

That familiar grunting, snuffling sound again and a slight rustle of wet vegetation. Hoover? Or whatever that damn thing was that followed her around? She wasn't naturally a superstitious person, but lying on a ledge in the shadowy otherworldly light, she hoped it was a living, breathing creature at least.

"Oh, for fuck's sake, don't be so lame," she muttered. "Of course it's flesh and blood, you idiot." For some reason her sharp, spoken out loud words buoyed her a little.

"Hoover," she called croakily, then managed a bit more volume. "Here, Hoover. Here, boy."

The rustling sound increased and there was a soft panting. "Hoover, I will kick your dog ass if you don't stop scaring the shit out of me!"

Yep, it really was pathetic. Talking tough to a pet that may or may not actually even be present was making her feel better, giving her a semblance of control.

And then, miracles of miracles, a canine snout *did* appear over the ledge, but it was long and narrow and a soft velvet black—a complete opposite of Hoover's wiry graying-brown muzzle. A pair of soulful brown eyes gazed down at her and for a surreal moment, Sam felt like the animal was Charlie's kindred spirit.

"You. Are. A. Moron," she snarl-whispered.

The dog whined.

"No, no, sorry. Not you."

They sat like that, the dog staring down at Sam, Sam staring up at her—or she assumed it was a female anyway—for a long minute. Suddenly she remembered her coffee and snack. Finally, one thing she'd managed to do right this whole stupid excursion. She'd packed a little food at least. Actually make that two things. She'd worn her bag around her neck and shoulder. It was safe on her body, unlike the phone. When she opened the bag, a small rattling sound further cheered her. *Three things*. She had a bottle of extra strength ibuprofen. Yay for menstruation and always being prepared for it to hit. (Now who'd have thought she'd ever get to say that, heh, heh.)

She swallowed two pills with her coffee that was now only slightly warmer than body temperature and took a handful of her precious almonds.

As she chewed them down, she opened her journal and scrawled the date and the words, "The peace of the great outdoors is sorely overrated—and there's not a glass of wine in sight."

Then she sighed heavily and wrote in slightly smaller letters, "I'm actually really scared, but I've survived worse and I will survive this." She underlined the last bit three times and stared at the words. She didn't write the next thought that came to her, but let herself curl into the knowledge and comfort of it. Her bold claim was true. She really had. She sometimes worried she was this hard, damaged person—but even if she kind of was, so what? Who wasn't in some ways? She was also someone who survived things and kept on keeping on. She was someone who went after what she wanted. She was not someone who sat on her butt and waited to be rescued. *If you don't like your situation, change it.*

She tucked the journal back into her bag and withdrew a large piece of jerky. As she tore off a chunk of the salty goodness with her teeth, the dog above her whined again.

"Of course," she said. "How rude of me." She took another piece of jerky and tossed it to the dog. It hovered feet short of the excited pink tongue and fell, rushing past Sam and plunging into the green water below her. She tried again. This time, success. The dog's long muzzle reached, jaws snapped and the jerky disappeared in a gulp.

Some people would say she was "wasting" her food, but a friend seemed more valuable than a few calories.

The dog barked once, sharply.

"You're welcome," Sam said.

A few droplets of rain splattered her face and she contemplated the sky again. Directly above her, the clouds were dull gray and sparse—but a heavy char-coal mass was rolling her way, moving quickly.

And it had been hours now. Was at the very least mid afternoon. If it rained hard all night or turned to wet snow as the temperature dropped, she'd be in worse trouble—and would have no chance at all of scaling the stupid rock face. And she'd just remem-bered her parting words to Callum about a long bath and shutting herself in. There was a good chance—and by good she meant terrible—that no one would look for her until the next day. But even then, if they did suppose she was missing, what would make them search in this direction?

Gritting her teeth, she scooted backwards and

braced herself on one of the rocks she'd banged her skull against. Haltingly, she made her way to standing. Don't look down, she commanded herself. Don't look. Her leg screamed. Her tailbone throbbed and sent out a sharp flare of pain . . . but she was on her feet. She tested her weight on her sore leg. Then raised her uninjured foot slightly off the ground. The fire in her leg burned so furiously she was instantly nauseated—but the leg held her.

"Thank you," she breathed.

Above her, the dog was practically lying over the cliff's edge, extended as close toward Sam as she could be, head resting on her front paws.

"Any chance you could pull a Lassie and run and tell Jo that Sammi's in the well?"

The dog tilted her head, as if seriously contemplating the question.

Sam sighed and leaned against the rocky wall. Everything in her wanted to sit back down, but she wasn't sure she'd make it to her feet again if she did.

What was the least stupid option? *What?*

A gust of wind kicked up, battering her lightly, then died. The ominous clouds scudded closer. Right now the rock face was dry at least. And standing upright revealed the path was considerably closer than it originally appeared, maybe only three or four feet above her head.

If she tried to climb and fell . . . wouldn't she just land back where she'd started? Or would falling from a different spot mean she'd land in a different spot too? Her gaze plummeted to the water so far below—

Stop it, she commanded.

She scanned the ridges above her and locked onto a long, weird, skinny tree—or maybe it was a root—growing, it seemed, right out of the rock itself. It was beyond her reach now, but if she could get up even one ledge, maybe . . .

A small plan started to form.

She adjusted her bag so it sat against her back not her hip, and turned to face the mountain. She reached as far as she could, straining her hands toward a sharp, knobby chunk of rock.

With a huff of relief and exertion, her hands closed around their intended marker. It seemed secure. She pushed off the ledge with her hurt leg, gripping her handhold with all her might and struggled to pull herself up, toes of her uninjured leg grappling for purchase. She found the ledge she sought and straightened on her good leg, panting. Her whole body shook with the effort she'd expended. She looked up. The dog peered down and seemed to smile. Slightly heartened by her already-much-closer face, Sam looked for the tree-root thing again. It was directly above her head. Would it work as the climbing rope she so desperately needed? She rested for another minute then reached out and latched onto the makeshift rope, doing her best to test its strength.

She only needed to get up two more ledges—or

three at the most—and then she'd be able to flop herself onto the path where her dog friend lay, keening encouragement.

Compared to the first, getting to the next ledge felt way easier. It wasn't as far a stretch, but she'd better move quickly. It was so narrow only her tiptoes rested on it. Not a good place to linger.

Just one more to go—or so she hoped.

The gap between the next ledge she needed and the one she perched on was further than she'd guesstimated. Her hands ached and were slick with sweat—or maybe rain as she noted in a slightly distanced way that fat droplets had started to fall.

Oh thank God, her toe found a niche. She bit her lip, tasted blood and hoisted her body up—

The spot her foot rested on let go and suddenly she was suspended, foot dangling. She bit back her scream. Gently scraped her foot side to side, feeling for *anything*. . . .

The toe of her boot found an edge again. She shuffled over a few inches to where it widened. Sweat beaded on her upper lip and she tasted salt.

She looked down the length of her body and went lightheaded with relief. A chunk of protruding shale created a perfect step only twelve inches or so from where she stood. It should be just enough to—

Still gripping the tree, she hoisted herself up, found the natural stair—and pushed off it, heaving forward. She crashed, sprawling to her stomach on the pine needled, rock-strewn ground. Her bag had propelled itself to her chest when she leapt, and the coffee mug burrowed into her ribs. Never had agony felt so good. The dog practically jumped on top of her, licking her face and whining. Sam couldn't make a sound, nor could she summon the energy or strength it would require to push the mutt off—and maybe she wouldn't have anyway.

She lay there with her living dog blanket for a long time, uncontrollable tears running down her face. When it had solidly registered that she was indeed on safe ground, she struggled onto her back, then up to sitting. Using her arms, she scooted back against a huge stump from which a younger tree grew hundreds of feet into the sky. It would provide some shelter at least.

She opened her bag. Ate more nuts. Ate more jerky—which again, she shared with the dog—a German shepherd or something, she noted, so skinny in the flanks and chest that she could see all her ribs. "Poor thing," she murmured and handed over more jerky. The dog grunted and took the offered food politely, which struck Sam as remarkable.

"So what now, Dog?"

Dog barked.

"No, I can't walk anymore. I don't even know how I got up here. It's impossible."

The dog barked again. Sam held her hands over her ears. "Stop that."

She looked down at her bag and an idea came to her . . . again, it may or may not work, but it was worth a try. She'd try to scrabble along the path, too, but in the meantime. . . . She swallowed her last two painkillers with the remains of the coffee, took her journal from her bag, tore out a piece of paper and scribbled, "Hey, it's Sam. I'm hurt on the trail to the canyon. Please come." Then she stuffed her journal into her shirt, and put the paper in the bag.

"Hey, Dog," Sam whispered. "Come on, girl." The timid animal belly-crawled closer, bribed by another scrap of jerky. Sam tied the bag around the dog's neck like a weird bib and was surprised when she didn't resist.

"Go home, Dog." She pushed at the shepherd.

Dog didn't move, just looked at her.

"Get going. *Go.*"

Still no movement.

Feeling like the worst person in the world, Sam picked up a small stone and shook it menacingly. "Go home."

Dog shook her head like Sam was crazy, trotted a few feet down the path, then stopped and looked back.

Sam's throat burned, but she threw the rock lightly. "Go!"

Dog's head bobbed once and she slunk away, disappearing into the bush almost immediately, leaving Sam alone in the gathering darkness.

She slumped back against the stump. You were

powerless against so many things that life threw at you. Could she have made better decisions various times throughout her life? Absolutely. Would some shit have happened to her regardless of what she chose? Absolutely again. But once the choices were made and you were left dealing with the consequences, perhaps that—how you dealt with them—was the only power you actually had. It was kind of encouraging, really. That she could choose how she reacted to things or let them affect her.

She straightened up a little, uncomfortable with her sagging spine. She had just climbed a rock face with a busted leg and she was what, going to quit now? Like hell! Yes, she was exhausted in some ways—but a second wind was building within her. It was like the cold seeping into her limbs from the ground was numbing her physical body but sharpening her mind. There was some nugget in all this thinking that applied to her and Charlie maybe, and it was something she'd explore—later, in her journal, wine in hand. For now, she had some more work to do.

Slowly, ignoring the creeping dark and the cold and the gnawing pain, Sam got to her feet again.

Chapter 22

CHARLIE WAS INCREASINGLY AGITATED AS the afternoon wore onto evening. He'd brought Aisha and Mo home from the hospital with no trauma or trouble and they'd spent a lovely afternoon together in Minnow cabin, where they were safely ensconced now as he paced the grounds around River's Sigh like a madman. Something wasn't sitting right with Sam's quick departure.

His questions the night before had irritated Sam—and he couldn't decide if that's because he'd poked a sensitive truth or because he was so wildly off base. Either way, he'd always expected her to take off unannounced sometime. It was a reality he'd tried to prepare Aisha for—one that even Jo, diplomatic as she was about Sam, didn't deny was a possibility.

But come on! Sam was also fearless about some things and passionate. He didn't for one second believe that her unvoiced, yet absolutely transparent affection for Aisha and the baby was feigned, so why would she leave without so much as a wave good-bye or a hint at where she could be found if needed? Did Aisha—did *he*—mean that little to her? No, he didn't believe it. But how else could you explain her taking off without leaving a trace she'd ever occupied Rainbow cabin with him? The SUV had been gone when he got up and hadn't returned once since. It was a long time for a mere outing. He hoped she'd just taken up residence in a hotel in town—but again, why not a word of it to anyone?

And by "anyone," you mean *you*, a voice in his head said—Sam's voice. It almost made him smile.

So where was she? Where was anyone? He hadn't seen hide or hair of Jo or Callum or any employees since he'd left to pick up Aisha. This place really was as isolated as Sam complained it was.

His phone pulsed then rang. He almost dropped it in his rush to answer. "Hello? Sam?"

"No, it's Evan. Is this Charlie?"

Evan. What the hell did he want? The kid obviously took his silence as an affirmative. "Can I please talk to Aisha?"

Charlie was shaking his head, even as he answered. "No, no you can't."

"Look, I know things aren't great between us—but I want to make amends with you, with her. I want to step up."

Charlie so didn't have the time or energy for more of the smarmy little bastard's ingratiating bullshit. He'd had his full of Evan Strait for a lifetime in the months Aisha had dated him. "It's not that. It's just she's not available. She just got home from the hospital."

"She had the—our—baby then? And she's home now?"

"Not home-*home*. We're still in Greenridge." Shit. The second the words were out, it occurred to him that Aisha may not have told Evan where she was living. He hoped he hadn't broken some taboo. For the millionth time he wished Aisha had been more forthcoming with specifics about what happened with Evan—but for all his gentle prodding, she wouldn't open up about it.

"Look, Evan. Whatever's gone on, it's between you and Aisha."

"But sir—"

"I'm sure she'll be in touch if it's the right thing to do. Good-bye, Evan."

Charlie ended the call, unable to shake the feeling he'd blundered, but still preoccupied with Sam's missing person status—okay, maybe that was a bit dramatic, but it didn't feel like it. He tried Jo's number again. And again, for like the fifteenth time, he got voicemail.

When the drizzle he'd been ignoring turned into a full-fledged downpour, he headed back to Rainbow. Sam wasn't his problem.

At the stairs, however, he hesitated, one hand on the railing, one foot on the first step. He stared at the tree line beyond the cabin. Where he stood it was still light, if dismal. The forest was already dark.

He turned abruptly, resolutely. Sam wasn't his "problem," true. But she was his friend. His good friend, whether she felt the same or not. And he couldn't—wouldn't—ignore his gut. He'd have done the same thing for a total stranger or even an enemy.

He was almost at Aisha's door, hoping to get Callum's cell number to see if he knew what Sam was up to, when the rustle of an animal in the brush startled him. Then he saw a blur of bright fabric. What the heck?

A large dog crept out of the shadows, acting half beaten and retreating as soon as Charlie tried to coax it forward. It was wearing something puffy around its neck and shoulder and Charlie shook his head. One of those dumb dog jackets, no doubt.

He called the dog one more time, planning to rescue it from its ill-fitted torture device, but the animal cowered and slunk from view. Charlie hesitated, but then continued on to Aisha's. He felt badly for the dog, but his worry for Sam had escalated.

Aisha was surprised to see him again so soon—and seemed like she'd been napping, which made him feel bad. His daughter had just had a baby. She needed her rest. Why was he troubling her with what was probably nothing?

"I was just, ah, wanting to know if you had Callum's number. I've tried Jo a zillion times, but get no answer. I haven't seen Sam all day."

Aisha studied him and her eyes seemed old. She shook her head. "Dad . . . you were the one who told me to expect this very thing. You said she wouldn't stick around."

"I know, I know. But something's off. I think I was wrong."

Aisha shrugged. "You warned me to be careful not to make her into something she's not. Heed your own advice."

Charlie scrubbed his hand over his face. What could he say? He had given that advice—and repeated it—even a few days ago, even when he knew full well that he was falling for Sam.

Oh, man, that was it, wasn't it? He really had fallen for her. Lot of good it would do him.

Aisha was talking again. "I don't have his number, but it's on the board by the phone in the office—and they usually leave the door unlocked." A shrill wail cut her off. "Oh, there's the eating machine. I have to go."

Charlie nodded and the door shut. He stood in the increasingly heavy rain another moment, then did the only thing he could. He headed for the office.

Chapter 23

BUT CHARLIE DIDN'T GET A chance to call Callum. Just as he was about to open the office door—which was indeed unlocked, a foolishly trusting move in his opinion—engines rumbled up the drive.

Jo's pickup arrived first, but Samantha's SUV was right on its bumper.

Jo raised her arm in a casual greeting before she got out of the truck, then she must've seen something that concerned her on Charlie's face because she bolted out the vehicle and ran toward him, boots splashing in the newly forming puddles.

"What's wrong?"

"Nothing, nothing," Charlie grumbled, embarrassed—then stopped talking as Callum climbed down from behind Sam's steering wheel. "Wait. Callum had Sam's vehicle?"

"Yeah," Callum said. "She said she didn't need it, that she was staying around the place all day. My car's in the shop."

"Well, she's not here. Hasn't been all day."

Callum looked uncomfortable and shook his head. "So she didn't tell you?"

"Didn't tell me what?"

"Silver was ready for her again," Jo added, but she was gazing toward Silver cabin with a slightly confused expression. "You haven't seen her at all? I thought she was planning to visit Aisha and the baby when they got home."

Charlie seethed at Jo's use of "home" to describe this place and realized he, like a selfish git, still felt as threatened by Aisha's choice as he ever had. "We thought that too, but she didn't show up. Didn't call. All her bags are gone and the SUV too—"

"So you assumed she'd taken off," Jo finished like it was a natural enough conclusion, but her brow furrowed. "It's strange there's not a single light on," she added.

Callum strode toward the dark cabin and knocked on the door. Charlie and Jo joined him on the porch. When there was no answer, Callum rapped again, harder.

Jo tested the doorknob. It was locked. "Sam?" she called. "Hey, Sam, you there?"

"You're sure you didn't see her?"

"Not once—and there haven't been any lights on in this cabin. I knew the previous guests had just moved out. I would've noticed."

Jo pulled a ring of keys from her pocket and fiddled with them to find the one she wanted. When she turned the lock, the door swung open. The space ahead of them gaped, still and quiet.

"Samantha? It's me. Jo." Jo flicked two switches by the door. The porch and the small foyer lit up. Sam's two massive suitcases sat rolled up against the granite topped kitchen island, and her laptop case and overnight bag were in plain view on the counter.

"What the . . ." But Jo didn't finish whatever she was going to say. She pulled out her cell phone, pressed a couple of buttons. "Sam, it's me. If you get this message call me back right away."

"I could've told you you'd get voicemail," Charlie said.

Jo glowered and Charlie was struck once more by the similarity between her, Sam's, and Aisha's faces. Callum slid his shoes off and headed into the depths of the cabin, opening doors and popping his head into each room as he did.

Jo pressed another couple buttons and chewed on the edge of her thumb while she waited for someone to pick up. "Hello—yes, Dave? It's Jo . . . no, the call's not social at all, sorry," she said flatly. "I was wondering if you'd seen Sam today or if she's with you by chance?"

Charlie held his breath during Dave's unheard response. His feeling of foreboding had intensified by the second since Callum had gotten out of Sam's vehicle, and now he was practically sick with worry. They were in the middle of nowhere with no one around. Anything could've happened. Anything at all. *Please let her be with Dave. Please let her be with Dave.*

"Okay . . . well, thanks. No, no need to worry, but hey, if she does call you, can you get her to contact me?"

Dave said something else.

"You bet. Thanks." Jo broke the connection and tapped her phone gently against her chin a few times. "He hasn't seen her," she said.

Charlie wanted to snarl, "Thanks, tips," but held his tongue. Jo wasn't her sister's keeper.

"Not a sign that she's been here since she stowed her luggage earlier," Callum said, returning to them.

"Shit," said Jo. "Shit, shit, shit."

"What?"

"Did she mention going for a walk or anything?"

Callum nodded. "Actually, she did—but a short one, and she's not the outdoorsy type. I can't see her going too far, or staying away too long."

"She's more into nature than you'd suspect," Jo contradicted.

Charlie had to agree. "She goes for long walks all the time."

Callum shrugged. "If you say so, but still . . ." He checked his phone for the time. "I saw her at like, nine thirty this morning. It's well after six now."

For the first time since Charlie had met her, true anxiety tightened Jo's features. "This isn't good. Sam would take off on an impromptu shopping trip or skip town for a holiday on whim—but she wouldn't disappear into the wilds on her own volition. Something's wrong."

It was amazing to Charlie how long it took people to arrive at the obvious sometimes. "That's what I've been saying the whole time!"

Callum and Jo both looked at him.

He held up his hands. "Sorry, sorry."

"I told her if she changed her mind about not needing a vehicle, you'd be home around lunchtime and she could use your truck. Maybe she got impatient and called for a cab or something," Callum said.

Jo's face scrunched and she smoothed her hand along the top of one of Sam's suitcases. "Nah, even if she'd decided there was something she was desperate for, she would've just called me. There was a place by the river she wanted to go back to though. I wonder—" She shook her head. "No, it would've been an intense hike even for someone who liked a lot of physical exertion."

"Sam's extremely fit," Charlie said, desperate for a place, any place, they could start looking, could do something, could stop just standing around.

"Well, yeah," Jo agreed, still being frustratingly slow to panic and get moving. "But she's gym fit. It's different."

"We're wasting time."

"I agree," Callum said and Charlie was glad he had

one ally at least.

"So let's grab flashlights and try the trail she and I took last time. If we don't find her within the hour, we'll call in somebody."

They headed back outside, leaving the lights on. Just as they cleared the porch, a sharp bark made them all jump. The bark came again, then a third time. As one, they turned toward the forest. All was black and shadows. And then there was movement in the tree line. At the very furthest reach of the light thrown from the porch, Charlie caught a flash of the dog in the ludicrous jacket-cape he'd seen earlier. And then there was a pale glimmer and a hunched human figure limped into view.

"So there's a welcoming committee. Excellent." The words were little more than breath, only audible because they were shocked to silence and the night was so still—but the voice was definitely Sam's.

Charlie didn't know who reacted first, him or Jo, but they were at Sam's side, becoming human crutches, almost instantly. As her arm drooped over his shoulder and she sagged against him, fury tore through Charlie, rendering him speechless.

Jo whispered a steady stream of encouragement and Callum ran ahead, back to Silver, muttering something about getting blankets ready and making broth. Charlie could only shake his head.

It wasn't until Sam was wrapped in a quilt and resting on the leather couch, with Jo carefully cutting the seam of Sam's pants to check out the injury, that Charlie found his voice. But he was horrified by what poured out. None of it was what he wanted to say.

"Of all the harebrained, idiotic, immature, unreasonable things to do. What were you thinking? Who runs off into the middle of bloody nowhere without saying a word to anyone?"

Sam's eyelids were heavy and her face was impossibly pale, but her mouth curved with a trace of her sardonic smile. "Sorry, Officer—but do you think the ticket can wait until we douse the fire in my leg? I'm thinking amputation might do the trick."

Jo gasped. "No, no, surely not." She resumed snipping the wet denim on Sam's leg with even greater urgency. "Shut the hell up, Charlie. *Shut up*." The anger in Jo's voice was as hot as his own.

But Charlie wasn't done. Not even close. All he could see is what could have happened, what had happened. . . . "What kind of selfish, arrogant asshole of a person are you? You're not invincible."

"Well, I almost am," Sam tried to joke.

"No, no one is. No one." Charlie's voice broke. "I told you a hundred times, *a hundred times*, to go the doctor, to get checked, but you kept putting it off and putting it off and then it was too late—"

Callum grabbed Charlie's shoulder roughly. "Come on, man. What are you on about? I think it's time for you to go."

Charlie's face flooded with heat, and he tapped his

clenched fist against his mouth. "I . . . I'm sorry. I—"

"Get him out of here," Jo said. "Please."

"Wait," Sam said wanly.

"No, you can talk to the—"

Whatever name Jo was going to call him was lost as Callum shoved Charlie out the door, then said, not unkindly, "Whatever you think this is, it's not—and you're not helping the situation any. Sam's banged up, but she'll be fine. You'll see."

The door clicked shut behind Charlie, the lock turned in the knob, then the deadbolt slid too. The rain hadn't let up and the cold was penetrating. What had he just done? Officially lost it? What was wrong with him?

A wavering howl filled the air. For a minute he thought the noise came from his own chest, and then he realized it was just that strange, lonely dog out of reach in the shadows.

Chapter 24

SAM HAD BEEN WAITING IN Emergency for five hours, and she was fed up.

"In the time it takes to see a doctor around here, I could actually develop a medical problem," she said, not bothering to whisper.

"Shhh, you're not funny. And maybe it's a good thing. If you were in dire straits they wouldn't keep bumping you for other patients."

"I've told you, it's not broken. I climbed on it and walked on it, for crying out loud."

"You're right. It's in perfect condition." They both looked down at Sam's foot where it protruded from the bottom of a fuzzy fleece nightgown she'd borrowed from Jo. It was swollen to almost triple its usual size right up to her knee, with no distinguishable ankle or toe knuckles or anything else. The really disturbing thing, however, was the color—her toes were an ugly blue-black and the rest of her foot was a mottled purplish green. "They did the monster mash," Sam sang under her breath and tried to wiggle her foot.

Jo cracked a smile, but then saw sweat pop out on Sam's brow at the effort. "Quit it!"

"Okay, fine. I admit having it looked at isn't the worst idea."

"They should check your head too."

"Oh, pshaw." Sam jostled Jo's arm. "You always say that."

Jo shook her head. "Whatever drugs you're on? They are gooood shit."

Sam grinned, but an icy shiver ran down her spine. The drug affecting her most, and she knew it without any pride or self-congratulations, was relief. It was a miracle she hadn't died, let alone survived with nothing more than—

"A greenstick fracture and a grade three sprain," the doctor confirmed when they finally got in to see her, showing them an X-ray and expressing mild shock and disapproval that Sam had walked on it.

"Didn't really have a choice," Sam muttered.

Later still, when Sam was sporting a fluorescent pink cast, the doctor snapped off her latex gloves and proceeded to bore Samantha with care details. Jo, however, seemed mesmerized, so Sam listened obligingly and even asked a question or two. Finally, though, she'd had enough. She agreed to see a GP in the next week and asked where to rent crutches.

"Come on, Jo," she whispered as the doctor went to a side counter and scribbled out two different prescriptions for painkillers. "Enough already. Let's get out of here. I have things to do."

"*Things*, hey? What on earth's so compelling that you can't stay another second to finish discussing your injury and recovery?"

Sam considered Charlie's rant and sighed. "Is there something else I should ask about?"

Jo's forehead creased. "No," she finally admitted. "You were a model patient."

"Good. So grab me some crutches and let's go."

IT WAS DAY TWO OF crutch-crap, but Sam had pretty much gotten the hang of using them by now. Her butt was numb and slightly damp from sitting on Silver's bottom porch step, but she'd gotten the damn dog to come so close she wasn't about to give up and go inside now. She opened the last weapon in her arsenal, wondering if she should've tried it first: beef jerky. She tore off a big piece and chewed it down herself. Then she held out a wad as near to the ground as she could manage with her casted leg stretched out in front of her.

"Here, Dog. Come on."

The black nose appeared from beneath the edge of the bushes again, but still didn't come any closer.

"You know you want it," she whispered. "Come on."

The dog—for the first time in the hour Sam had

been out there—slid her whole body out of hiding and inched forward on her belly.

"You poor thing, we've already met. You should know I won't hurt you." Sam broke off a tiny piece of jerky and tossed it. The dog had to move forward another inch or two to snap it up. Sam repeated the motion twice. The dog went for the jerky each time. It was only feet away from her now, but stayed low to the ground, ready to flee. Sam set a large tempting piece at her feet. Then had an idea. It might scare the dog at first, but in the end . . .

She scrabbled to her feet, got her crutches under her, and maneuvered into the cabin, leaving a trail of well-spaced jerky tidbits behind her. She hoped Jo wouldn't mind her trapping a dog in there. And if the animal went nuts? Oh well, she'd just pay for any cleaning or repairs.

She propped herself behind the open door and waited. For a long moment she thought she'd failed and then Dog started to move. Slowly at first, then with more confidence. She halted at the threshold, however, and Sam held her breath. But the pile of jerky sitting three feet into the entrance was more temptation than Dog could bear. She lunged inside—

Sam quickly shut the door. Dog startled—but made quick work of the jerky pile. Bizarrely, now that she was trapped, she didn't seem that perturbed. And up close, Sam was able to see just how badly in need of care she actually was. She turned away from the animal and crutch-walked to the counter where she had readied dishes of water and canned food earlier, just in case.

She talked the whole time she moved, not loudly, not quietly, just matter-of-factly. "You look hungry so I took the chance. Hope you like chicken. You definitely need fattening up. And a vet. And—whew—a bath. You reek like a dog."

Although Sam kept her back turned, she sensed the dog watching her, listening to every word. She put the food down by the island—quite a feat on crutches—then walked to the living room, giving the dog the widest berth possible, and settled on the couch.

She then tried to ignore the animal for all she was worth, and flipped through a magazine. A few minutes passed—and then she heard greedy gulps and chews. Dog practically inhaled her food. But Sam only knew she'd succeeded when, after a few minutes of pacing and a whine or two, Dog curled into a ball in the corner of the dining room. Yes, she'd settled as far away from Sam as she could, but settled she had. It was huge.

Sam pulled out her new replacement phone and entered Jo's number.

"Guess what I just got?" she asked when Jo answered.

"What?"

"A dog!"

"What? Is that why you were so urgent about shopping yesterday? You were buying dog stuff?"

Sam laughed. "Yep. Come visit after lunch. I want your opinion."

"Callum can eat alone today." Jo was over in minutes.

Dog didn't fuss when Sam opened the door, but she took off, skittering across the kitchen and hightailing it for the living room when Jo entered.

"I don't know, Sam." Jo crouched and studied the dog cowering between the recliner and the wall. Dog showed her teeth but didn't growl, and Jo straightened up. "She seems pretty wild, and in pretty bad shape. If you want a dog, this might not be the best—"

"I don't want 'a' dog. I want Dog."

"You named her 'Dog'?"

Sam nodded.

"What a heartwarming, cuddly name."

"It's ironic."

Jo laughed. "Of course it is."

"So can I keep her?"

"Are you, like . . . asking my *permission*?"

"Well, I'm going to be staying here for a while and . . ."

Jo patted Sam's shoulder. "Of course you can keep Dog here, and who knows? You might be the perfect owner for her. It's a big commitment though, and when you travel and stuff—"

"We'll cross those bridges when we come to them. Don't you think she's beautiful?"

Jo looked at the dog again. "I do actually."

"She just needs some TLC—and to get used to life and people not kicking the crap out of her."

"You think she's been abused?"

Sam cocked her head and gave her new pet an appraising look. "I don't know. Abused or neglected—or maybe she just got lost and never found her way back. In some ways it doesn't matter what happened in the past, she's in a good place now."

Jo was staring at her, wide-eyed—almost like she was worried. A zing of apprehension tingled through Sam. "What? What's wrong?"

Jo shook her head. "Nothing, nothing. I just . . . you seem different. That's all." Sam snorted. "Don't worry. I'm not. Why mess with perfection?"

"Yeah . . . why indeed?" Jo asked but she still seemed lost in thought, even as she agreed that yes, Dog should definitely see a vet and, even more surprisingly, didn't argue at Sam's insistence to pay a higher nightly rate since she had a pet now.

Jo headed out. Dog waited a good ten minutes to be sure the terror had actually left the building, then took over the mat in front of the door as if to ward off any other unwanted intrusions. Sam fidgeted with her phone. It had been fun talking to Jo about Dog, but— and she felt irritated and anxious at the realization— who she really wanted to tell, who she really wanted to see, was Charlie. But would he still be off his rocker with rage when she saw him, or were they still friends? If they weren't, well, fine. He was half-lunatic anyway.

So why did her stomach feel like a mess of coiling snakes at the idea that maybe they weren't on speaking terms anymore and maybe she wouldn't get to share Dog with him?

Chapter 25

CHARLIE WAS SEATED AT THE small kitchen table, laptop in front of him all but forgotten. He stared down at his cell phone, and hit a button to listen to Sam's message again. He was dying to see her—and mortified at the very idea. He wasn't exactly sure what had happened in his head the other evening, but it was probably as close to a breakdown as he'd ever had.

She sounded chipper in the voicemail initially, excited about some surprise she had for him, then her voice had lowered. "And well, we should probably talk about how we left things the other night."

How they'd left things the other night. Did she mean like, between the two of them the last night they'd fooled around and had dinner, etc., etc., or did she mean the other night as in three nights ago when she'd found her way back to River's Sigh bruised and beaten up, and he'd lost his shit on her?

He sighed heavily. There was only one way to find out, and despite the embarrassment boiling his blood as he tried to figure out what to say in apology, his mind buzzed with happy anticipation. Whether she'd written him off as relationship material for good or not, she'd invited him over to her cabin and she had a surprise for him. At least he was getting to spend time with her again.

He sent a quick text saying he'd be right over—actually, that he'd love to come right over. And what the heck, it was the truth.

"Are you sure you're up to this?" he found himself asking a few minutes later.

"Absolutely, and Dog needs to walk."

"Dog"—the funniest name for a dog Charlie had ever heard—growled low in her throat as Sam transferred the leash to Charlie, and continued to make angry, complaining sounds the whole time they trekked around the perimeter of the parking area and down the driveway. Sam's speed surprised Charlie. She moved so swiftly over the damp gravel, it was like the crutches were an extension of her body.

"You're pretty good on those."

Sam gave a one-shouldered shrug. "Now. You should've seen me day one and two."

"Yeah, about that . . . I'm sorry I didn't come by to see how you were doing."

They were both quiet for a bit and Charlie wondered what she was thinking. Had she just invited him along to manage the dog, or was it something else?

Sam paused and took a deep breath. "It sure smells good, hey? Pine and rain and running sap. . . ."

Charlie stopped walking. "It sure does, but be careful. You're dragging me on a walk, commenting on the fresh air. . . . You hurt yourself *hiking*. If you don't watch it, I'm going to start thinking that you, Samantha Kendall, are becoming a lover of the great outdoors."

"Let's not get too crazy. I was complimenting the air quality, not writing a sonnet."

Charlie laughed.

They were about halfway down the long driveway that led to the highway when Samantha waved a crutch at something nearby. "Okay, I need a rest."

Charlie glanced where she pointed and noted a huge fallen log. He strode over to check whether she'd be able to handle the terrain between it and the road, gave a nod, and headed back to help her.

Moments later, they were sitting on the furthest end of the log, deepest into the forest. Sheltered by a huge sweeping bough of ancient greenery, the spot was remarkably dry and private.

Sam took the leash back, Dog finally quit complaining and settled into a doughnut shape in the crook between the log and the ground. "In another few weeks, when the undergrowth greens up, this place will be invisible to the road, but it will still be here. A perfect refuge, even if no one but us knows about it."

Charlie took her hand like it was something he did all the time, and looked down at the bandages protecting her scraped up palm. He had no idea how to reply, but her words sparked a tiny flare of hope. What was she saying?

She was squinting off into some unseen place in the distance when she spoke again. "So here's the thing. I haven't been quite honest with myself—or with you. I do want you, Charlie. In a way I find a little terrifying actually."

He had to refrain from tightening his grasp on her sensitive hand.

"And it occurred to me while I was attempting to keep my dumb ass alive that it's not like me to not go for what I want."

He could hardly breathe for the joy forming a huge lump in his throat, and he calmed himself by rubbing her wrist with his thumb.

"I have no idea if we'll work out long term as you so optimistically think we might." He opened his mouth to speak, but she pushed on before he could. "But it's worth trying if you can figure out some things. One, if you're really over Maureen—"

A pained gasp escaped him and he realized he'd been holding his breath.

Sam's expression was tender and her eyes were as green as the cedar boughs around them as they reflected the light. "Oh, I know you still love her and always will—and that's fine. But that transference crap, you taking issues you had with her out on me. I'm not in. I like to be the high maintenance one in a relationship."

Charlie laughed, even as he winced. "Yeah, about that—"

"No, save the apology. I get it. The stress of the situation came to a head when I turned up all right, but the ramifications of what could have happened over-whelmed you, triggered memories, blah, blah, blah."

"Wait, *what*?" It definitely wasn't normal to be grinning like a fool and trying to fight off a laugh when you were having your ass nailed to the ground in some slightly derisive—though pretty spot on—pseudo-psychoanalysis, but he couldn't help it. Would her astringent wit always make him laugh or would he tire of it one day? He hoped he got the opportunity to find out.

"Two. You have to figure out how to make it okay with Aisha. If you can get her blessing, I'm in. If not . . . " She shrugged again.

"It shouldn't matter what Aisha thinks."

"Don't be daft. Of course it does. I have less than no interest in coming between you guys or being some hated stepmother-slash-bio mom. It's too weird." She gently untangled her fingers from his. "And don't kid yourself either. I've seen you with her and Mo. You were furious with me before you even knew me, thinking I'd come between you guys or wreck your relationship. Don't think you'll be any less devastated if you willingly choose the same result."

Charlie frowned. Sam braced one of her crutches against the heavily pine-needled forest floor and heaved herself to standing. This time she retained her grip on Dog's leash, looping it around her uninjured

EV BISHOP

palm and holding it against the foam hand rest.

"Look," Sam said softly. "Some people say you can never truly lose someone you've loved, that relationships just change is all—but you and I both know that's a load of crap. Of course you can lose someone—by death, by betrayal, by plain old miscommunication and misunderstandings . . . and memories are pretty skimpy consolation."

Charlie stood up to accompany Sam back, but she shook her head. "I can get back by myself if you want to think for a bit."

"All right." He watched Sam hop-march away from him and a flurry of emotions moved through him. What had she just offered him? And was she right, would choosing her cost him his daughter? Surely not. Aisha had always been mature for her age. She'd understand he and Sam hadn't planned any of this. She'd want him to take a shot at being happy again, wouldn't she?

A memory of the expression in Aisha's eyes the night Sam was missing flashed through his mind, however, and her words repeated in his head, *Be careful not to make her into something she's not. Heed your own advice.*

Had his advice been wise or not—and was Aisha's reference to it helpful or the opposite of that? He was suddenly unsure.

Sam's face appeared before him with such clarity he felt he could reach out and stroke her cheek. Before

232

today, he'd thought she was the one holding back, the one who wasn't sure she wanted a relationship, but their talk—and her pointed questions—made it all too clear. It wasn't Sam who was hesitant. He'd just used her as an excuse. Maybe he'd chosen her because an unconscious part of him was sure she was unavailable. How damaged was that? But had he, could he, truly let Maureen go? And would he let himself love someone who might create a barrier between him and his daughter? The idea stunned him. *Love*. That really was what he felt for Samantha, though they hadn't known each other long enough and the situation was a mess. Love.

A few years back Charlie would've said, "Well, that's it then. That solves everything." But now? Well, now, despite his thoughts the other night to Maureen about what he wanted to believe, he knew all too well—and knew Sam knew too—love wasn't always enough. And it came with so much risk attached. He didn't know if he was up to it anymore.

"So I'll just tell her that," he muttered. That was another good thing about Sam. She had such low opinions of people, she wouldn't be shocked he was spineless. He smiled as he lumbered to his feet and moved away from the log. She did make him miss the old days when he'd had a backbone—and that was something pretty great.

He walked back toward River's Sigh, noticing the sweet air, the promise of heat to come, and the richness of life in a way he hadn't during spring since Maureen's passing. With every step he took, his optimism grew.

Optimism that crashed at the scene that greeted him just outside Sam's SUV.

Chapter 26

AISHA WAS IN A RAGE. Her eyes and face practically sparked with negative energy and she was pointing at Sam and yelling. Sam was flattened against the side of her vehicle, looking little and frail on her crutches—two adjectives he'd never in a million years usually associate with Sam. Dog was nowhere to be seen.

Charlie ran toward the two women.

"I'm sorry," Sam was saying. "I had no idea—well, obviously it was a big deal, yes. I'm sorry."

"You had no right. No fucking right at all!"

Charlie was slightly startled to hear the F-word out of Aisha's mouth, not that he was naïve. He figured she swore occasionally. Just not usually around him. But it was her temper that shocked him. Aisha was impassioned about things, absolutely, and dramatic, but she wasn't . . . mean.

"You didn't want to meet and you were right. Not meeting would've been best. And ever since we first shook hands, you've kept saying you won't hang around long. Make good on that promise. Get away from me and Mo and stay away. Our lives are none of your business!"

Sam's face was calm but sad, and she was nodding like Aisha's rant actually made some sort of sense. She glanced at Charlie as he approached and gave a slight jerk of her chin, telling him "No" about something, but he had no clue about what.

"I'm sorry," Sam repeated. "It must be really hard for you that Evan has showed up. I—I had no idea this would happen."

"Bullshit, bullshit, bullshit," Aisha exploded—then all the bluster went out of her voice like a balloon that's been let go. She was defeated and tired sounding. "I . . . I just thought you of all people would understand."

Sam leaned one of her crutches against the SUV and stretched her hand out toward Aisha. "I do and I'm sorry that—"

Aisha jerked away from Sam's touch, her jaw tight and mouth hard. She seemed to notice Charlie for the first time. "You were right about her, Dad. In every way. I wish we'd never met." Her furious glare stabbed Sam again. "If you go tonight it's not too soon."

"Aisha?" Charlie finally found his voice. "What on earth—"

"What's going on?" Jo interrupted, coming up behind them. "What's all the yelling about?" Her voice trailed off as she took in Aisha and Sam's faces.

Sam gripped her crutch again. "The kid and I were

just saying good-bye."

"What?" Jo said. "Just like that? I thought you were going to stay around, or be closer at least."

Sam shrugged. Charlie's heart twanged. How had he ever thought she managed to pull off nonchalance? The masks Sam slipped on were so obviously that— *masks*. His chest constricted, interrupting his own thoughts as he suddenly realized what must have happened. In the upheaval of the past few days, the rush of his writing going well, and visiting little Mo whenever he could, he'd totally forgotten about Evan's call. What an idiot he'd been—what a colossal idiot. "Wait a minute. Aisha, it's not—"

Sam cut him off. "Charlie, don't. It's not worth it."

Jo's eyebrows rose so high they almost disappeared off her face, and she held up her hand when he tried to respond to Sam. "*Not worth it*? How can you say that? You're a grandma now—"

Aisha scoffed. "Biologically maybe. It's not like she's a real one."

"Aisha!" Jo hissed.

"She left me before, thank God. She should leave me in peace now."

Sam's mouth fell open slightly and she inhaled like she'd just been slapped, but Charlie seemed to be the only one who saw her hurt.

He was at her side in a blink and went to wrap his arm around her. She shook him off and her voice was cuttingly casual. She even smiled. "Sure thing. No problem. I'll see you in another decade or two maybe."

Charlie stared into Sam's face, then pointed wordlessly at Mo, a sleeping bundle of purple and yellow in the baby carrier, just paces away from the meltdown of her family. Sam's eyes widened, but her lips compressed. She wouldn't follow his gesture. "It answers question number two, hey? And it's okay, Charlie. It's better this way."

Aisha turned, scooped up the baby carrier's handle, and strode away without so much as a backward glance.

Sam's body wilted beside Charlie and this time she didn't refuse his arm.

Jo's sharp words stopped her. "What the hell, Sam?"

"What do you mean?"

Jo rubbed her hands over her face, opened her mouth, then shut it again, and followed Aisha.

Sam lowered her head and didn't say a word.

Charlie put his hands on Sam's hips and pulled her to him, then leaned his cheek on the top of her head. She nestled close. "I appreciate what you tried to do there," he whispered against her silken hair, "but no way. I'm not letting you take the blame for my big mouth. I just thought—"

Sam's chin rubbed back and forth against his chest as she shook her head. "No," she said, voice muffled. "Aisha's right. It was her place to tell Evan anything or nothing. He had his chance. He blew it."

"I know, I know—I kicked myself the minute I gave away her location, but he called the day you were missing and my head was a mess and . . . I just wasn't thinking. He sounded so sincere. Said he just wanted to talk to her. Said he wanted to step up."

"Yeah, talk. *Step up.* Good one. Anyway, it's a big mess. Let her think it was me. She needs you. And she needs you to be the dad she thinks you are."

"But I still don't get it. Why does she think it was you anyway?"

Sam sighed. "It seemed like the easiest thing—no, false. It seemed like it might spare you some heat, and I didn't actually lie. I just . . . didn't overtly state that it wasn't me. She came out, guns blazing, asking who had 'blabbed' to Evan. She assumed he called the bed-and-breakfast, and since I took phone duty for a few hours the other day, I guess I was the logical choice."

"Well, I'm telling her the truth immediately. And on that note, I was coming here to say I don't need to think. I want to see what we have. I want to pursue—"

Sam pulled back and looked up at him. "You have so much, and you'll have love again too. Pick someone better suited to you and your family."

"But I want you. And you said you wanted me— and that it's not like you to not go for what you want."

Sam laughed but as she did the wind picked up and the sound was lost in the shaking of bare, desolate branches that had yet to bud. "I also know when to cut my losses. Ask Jo. She'll tell you. But you already knew that. And whatever else you said when you warned Aisha about me was probably true, too."

"No."

Sam rubbed the stubble along his jaw, then rested her fingertips on his mouth. "Don't feel bad. It's just not our time. We helped each other, though. Now you know you're ready to let someone else into your life—"

"Not someone, no. *You.*"

Sam bit her lip and a small, choked sound escaped her before she continued. "And you've shown me that I want more, or different things, at least, than I've had before."

"No," Charlie repeated for the umpteenth time. "We can't end this way. We can't."

"Silly, Charlie, of course we can. We hadn't even really started yet."

Charlie hated how Sam's saucy smile made his blood thrum even while the heart pumping it was breaking. She was already rebuilding the wall between them, and there wasn't a single thing he could do about it.

Charlie opened his mouth to argue and just a hint of the softness he'd learned to recognize in Sam showed in her face, but her voice and words were firm as stone. "Go." She jerked her chin in the direction of the cabin. "Help our—your daughter. The little dirt bag Evan made noises about trying to get custody."

Charlie jolted and turned away from Sam despite himself. He took three hesitant steps toward Minnow, then faltered. The end of Sam's crutch pressed against his lower back, giving permission for him to move on, nudging him to do so, in fact.

Chapter 27

SAM WATCHED CHARLIE LEAVE AND held her tongue though every part of her body practically screamed for him not to go. She marveled at this connection they seemed to have forged and hoped not seeing it through, not seeing what they might have had, wouldn't set either of them back too badly. Chickening out and choosing the path of least resistance was a loser move, no doubt about it, especially in light of her freshly forged vow to be brave and to go after what she wanted even if it scared the crap out of her.

How long had it taken her to go back on her own promise to herself? An hour? Awesome. Ah, well. It didn't matter. Deep down she knew—she'd always known—she wasn't someone who'd get the sweet, easy home life portrayed in TV sitcoms and cleaning commercials. Really, nobody did. Look at what she'd planned for Aisha all those years ago and how her life had turned out. Motherless as Sam had always felt. Raising a kid alone if she was lucky, or with a dead-beat dad in the picture if she wasn't. A good brain, but no formal education plans. She'd have to grovel her way out of scraping ends together just the way Sam had—

No. Sam pushed the false impressions away, gripped her crutches and started moving. Aisha had a great life, or the potential for one anyway. She made her choices, and had the strength of conviction to see those choices through. Maureen, by all accounts, had been a loving mom who'd raised a take-no-shit kid, and Sam was happy for that. Aisha was strong. She got angry and motivated when hurt; she didn't roll up into a corner and wait for other people to help her or tell her what to do. And as for Aisha being motherless. Well, she really couldn't hold Maureen responsible for dying, even if she wanted to—and apparently Charlie kind of did, too. *Charlie.*

She sighed heavily and continued her lurching march toward Silver. She'd pack and leave tonight. Aisha was right. Why put off what was inevitable? Charlie would clear up the misunderstanding sooner or later. It wasn't his nature to lie. He was an open book with all his emotions. One of the things she loved about him. Love! What a useless, tiresome, hurtful emotion that was. But even when it was cleared up and Aisha knew it was Charlie who had inadvertently informed Evan of Aisha and Mo's whereabouts, it wouldn't change the fact that Aisha was right. Who was Sam to them, really? Why should she get to be in their life?

Sam was on the porch now. Behind the door Dog was making high-pitched you're-finally-home noises, even though she'd only been locked up for what, thirty minutes? Sam was about to turn the key in the locked handle when Jo approached.

"I'll help you pack."

Sam pivoted toward her. "Just like that? You'll help me pack."

"Yep."

Sam faced the door again, opened it a crack so Dog wouldn't escape, and slipped inside.

It didn't take long. Sam felt she'd barely had time to blink and Jo had placed the last suitcase into the Mercedes and was slamming the door.

"So . . . " Sam said.

"So . . . " Jo echoed, then stretched her arms and looked up at the sky. "There are a few hours of light left, and it's not raining. No clients are booked for tonight—well, except Charlie and he doesn't count. Want to hit the creek with me one more time?"

Dog stood perfectly still on her leash, then made an excited whining sound like she understood what Jo was asking and voted yes. Or maybe, Sam rethought her notion, she just wanted to play with Hoover. The mutt, never far from Jo's side, had just appeared around the edge of the cabin, nose to the ground like he was on the trail of something delicious. Good grief, Sam thought. I just spent time imagining what might or might not be going through my dog's head. I'll be as nuts as Jo soon.

And speaking of Jo: her sister was staring at her with a concerned expression. "What is going on with you?"

"You wouldn't believe me if I told you," Sam mumbled.

"Try me."

Sam laughed. "No, but I will go fishing with you one last time. If you think I can manage it without breaking my other leg, that is."

The blue-green pool was untroubled and still. Just paces away, however, the creek frothed and pulsed. It was funny to Sam how the deep calm and the frenetic rushing were part and parcel of the same stream.

She followed Jo's steps and rigged her own fishing rod.

"This time you're using my lucky wedding band," Jo said like she was doing her an enormous favor.

Sam rolled her eyes, but when she cast her line a minute later—after a few reminder tips from Jo—she was surprised at the delight that rippled through her. It was like her body remembered what to do from last time. The lure and line swished out, then fell in a perfect arc far from the shore.

Jo whistled. "Nicely done."

Her lure had only been in the water for seconds, literally, when Sam felt a strong tug. "Oh no," she said. "Oh no."

"What's oh no? What's wrong?"

"I think"—her rod jerked again, stronger this time—"I think I have a fish on."

"That's not an oh no, that's an oh yay!" Jo reeled in her own line, grabbed a small net, and sprinted over to Sam.

There was a splash and a flash of silver and then another.

"It's a beautiful little rainbow trout from the looks of it," Jo said.

The fish danced again, lifting out of the river in a spray of droplets, its sides glinting metallic green and purple with tiny black dots.

Sam winced, then sighed heavily. "It's so pretty."

"It is—" Jo darted a glance at Sam. "What's wrong?"

"I . . . I just thought I'd go fishing with you like last time. Not that I'd actually catch anything." The fish disappeared beneath the surface and the tension on Sam's rod eased. "It's getting tired of fighting."

"They do that," Jo said softly.

"Can I let it go? Catch and release? That's a thing, right?"

"Of course. Reel in hard now, fast—but smooth."

Sam complied.

And suddenly the fish was at the edge of the bank and Jo was in the water with it, grabbing it firmly and pulling it out.

Held fast in Jo's iron grip, the trout seemed to stare up at Sam, its glittering sides flexing, its gills heaving but getting no oxygen. "Don't worry, Sam. It's a barbless hook." Jo reached into the gaping mouth and made a small movement Sam couldn't quite see. "She'll be fine."

The fish slipped off the hook as if to prove Jo's words, but then wallowed, inert, in the shallows.

"Oh no—"

"She's fine. Just needs a little prompting, that's all. Grab her tail and swish her lightly." Sam did as bidden and was shocked when touching the fish wasn't as disgusting as she'd feared. At her touch, the fish wiggled a little—then strained away. Sam let go. Silver flashed—and the trout disappeared into a deeper, safer place.

She stared at the swirl of silt and bubbles in the disturbed water. "Wow, that was really something," she said finally.

Jo nodded and handed her rod back.

"Nah, I'm good for now. You fish. I'll watch."

"No, I'm good too."

They leaned their rods on a log and settled themselves on a huge white rock. Jo opened a thermos of hot chocolate and poured them each a small stainless steel mug full.

Sam inhaled deeply. It was weird how she was never bored here—and with nary a shoe store in sight, ha ha.

"Okay, I admit it," she said breaking the soft green-gray silence. "You have something really good. I understand how a person could get hooked."

"Hooked on life here, or hooked on Charlie?"

Sam sipped her cocoa, didn't reply.

"I thought so," Jo said triumphantly. "So why not stay? You could rent Silver permanently for a reduced rate or buy a place in town—"

"It's tempting."

"So give in."

Sam closed her eyes briefly. She'd thought she and Jo would have this conversation with her computer nearby and notes in hand—the lovely, reliable numbers there to lean on and support her—but maybe this was better. It would be a different type of venture for Sam, so it might as well be set apart right from the start. She opened her eyes again. "I'd actually wanted to talk to you, well, to you and Callum, about bringing me in as a partner."

"What?"

"You heard me," Sam said, smiling—but then Aisha's angry face flared in her memory and she faltered. "But, well, maybe if Aisha's serious about staying on long-term I need to give it more thought."

Jo looked out across the river and her focus was on some unseen point in the distance when she spoke. "We're doing fine, Sam. Totally fine. We don't need—"

"No," Sam broke in. "You're doing *great*, actually. My interest isn't thinly veiled criticism. It's a bit selfish as usual." Her voice dropped so low it was difficult to hear, even for herself. "Let's just say I'm starting to understand your obsession about building something tangible."

Jo's eyes snapped to Sam's face.

Sam shrugged and nodded.

Jo shook her head. "You do need to think about this more—not because we wouldn't be grateful and couldn't benefit from your help, but because it might be an anchor you don't appreciate, whether Aisha's on the scene or not. And about Aisha. She's great, but I'm not choosing her over you. There will always be a place here for her and Mo, but there will always be one for you, too—and that's something she'll have to grow up about."

Sam harrumphed lightly.

"And for what it's worth, Sam, what you did back there was bullshit."

"What do you mean?"

"Don't widen your eyes and play innocent with me. I always know that's the furthest thing from what you are."

Sam laughed a little.

"There's no way you went behind Aisha's back to Evan. None. And if she wasn't awash in postpartum hormones and half insane with sleep deprivation, even though she doesn't know you super well, she'd know that."

"Well—"

"No, I'm serious. It was stupid and dishonest—two things you rarely are—for you to cover for Charlie."

Sam shrugged. "He's her dad and he's a good guy, motivated by good intentions."

"So not the point."

"We'll have to agree to disagree. What I wanted to talk about was me fronting you the money to renovate those unfinished cabins in the back and to build more. I think you could run this place at full capacity, even if you had twenty cabins."

Jo yelped and held up her hands. "Beware of blessings that are actually curses."

"Too daunting a workload?"

"Twenty yes, but twelve. . . ."

"Well, we'll talk more later. Run it by Callum. He might not want me involved. If he does, we can flesh out concrete details then."

Jo swallowed the rest of her cocoa. "So you'd be a silent partner."

Sam hesitated, and then straightened her shoulders. "Absolutely. Just a straight up loan, paid back with interest or maybe some deal with profit sharing down the road. It's an investment, that's all. That's my way. You know."

Jo studied Sam's face. "Wow."

Sam shrugged and gave her best cool gaze in return.

"When you said you wanted to 'build something tangible,' you meant you were thinking of being involved-*involved*, weren't you? Like taking part in the day-to-day running of River's Sigh?" Jo stood, shoved her and Sam's mugs into her backpack, and hefted the rods.

"Maybe I was . . . just a little, in the high season." Sam shimmied herself up to standing, too. "But recent developments—" She cleared her throat. "Well, let's just say I've realized a simple cash injection might be best."

Jo walked the trail ahead of Sam, keeping a brisk pace and not babying Sam because of her injury. Sam appreciated it just as much as she did *not* appreciate the lecture she knew was coming.

"Look, I know you don't want to hear this, but I need to say it."

Could she call it or what?

Jo continued. "People betray you. It's the problem with having family—any loved ones at all, actually. They open you wide up for potential pain, and facing the truth that they could be lost can make you freakishly possessive and insecure. But the flipside is that nothing else in life offers the happiness, peace and deep joy that letting people in, letting them love you— and letting yourself love them back—does. You know it's true from all the investing and trading you've done: reaping a reward always demands a level of risk."

"Yeah, well," Sam said, panting a bit from the effort of speed walking and trying to talk while on crutches. "Plenty of people lose their shirts and end up in the poorhouse too—and that analogy works both ways just like yours does."

"Bah. There are smart risks and idiot risks. You know that and you know the difference."

"Wait a minute. What are you getting at? Are you talking about me partnering with you and Callum or do you mean Charlie?"

Jo stopped so abruptly that Sam bumped into her. "Hey!" She tapped Jo's calf with her crutch. "Don't do that. I can't make fast stops."

"Of course I was talking about Charlie."

"Well, Charlie's off the table. But backing you isn't. Ask Callum if he's interested in a silent partner."

Jo resumed walking and gave no yea or nay.

Chapter 28

THE LIGHT SHE AND JO had enjoyed at the river was disappearing, and the tree line zipping past was a moody black-green streak beneath the leaden sky.

Her cell phone pulsed. She looked at the call display, sighed, and turned it facedown on the passenger seat. Charlie yet again.

"You want to end up dead? Keep your eyes on the road, dummy," she muttered aloud. Behind her, the desolate highway was empty as far as the eye could see—something she knew because she kept checking the rearview mirror again and again and again: obsessive even by her own high level of tolerance for such behavior.

She took a turn too fast, saw a road sign announcing the distances to the next three towns, then hit the brakes so hard she practically did a brake stand. Shaken, she pulled over to the gravel shoulder. She'd been hit with a memory from the day she'd fallen into the canyon—and how she'd felt in those exhausted hours. All she'd wanted was to give up and wait to be rescued, but she hadn't. She'd decided, as ever, that no, she needed to walk out on her own.

She always wanted to be that lone cowboy, secure and safe and able to survive alone—and there was strength in that, absolutely. But there was loneliness too. And she didn't want to be lonely anymore.

Her vow from that night came back to her. She'd promised herself that she'd think how the lessons she'd learned there might apply to her and Charlie—but she'd only gone halfway, hadn't she? She'd made a pretense of bravery when they'd talked on that log— only to back away from that resolve, let her nerve fail her, in the face of Aisha's disapproval.

She killed the engine, folded her arms over the steering wheel, and dropped her head.

Finally, after a long time, when the air inside the vehicle had cooled around her, she lifted her face, restarted the SUV, did a three-point-turn and slowly drove back the way she had come.

Charlie's Toyota was nowhere to be seen when Sam pulled back into River's Sigh, but that was just as well for now. She parked as close to Minnow cabin as she could, climbed out of the Mercedes and let Dog out to roam, then bolted toward Aisha's door as quickly as her crutches would let her, determined not to lose her nerve.

Sam knuckles had barely graced the door when it flew open. She took a step back as Aisha's disembodied voice blurted crossly, "What do you want now? I said I was sorry already. I feel terrible, all right?"

"All right with me," Sam said breezily. "But who'd you say sorry to?"

There was a split second of stony silence, then Aisha stepped into view from behind the door. "Sam," she said.

"In the flesh."

Aisha's complexion was butter yellow and her hair looked unnaturally amber in golden glow of the lamp above the door—but for all that heightened, surreal color, her expression was pale and stressed. "I thought you were my dad."

"I figured." There was another moment of strained silence. "May I come in?"

Wordlessly, Aisha moved back and opened the door wider.

Sam crutch-clomped into the tiny living room, smiled down at dozing Maureen and eased herself into an armchair. "That kid will sleep through anything, hey?"

"Yeah." Aisha's face creased in a tentative smile, and she perched on the edge of a wooden stool near the island counter that served as the small area's sole dining space. "Look," she started. "About that stuff I said, about you, about Evan—"

Sam waved her hand. "Don't worry about it. It's forgotten."

Aisha shook her head. "Not good enough, but thank you. I have to apologize. I am sorry, for whatever it's worth."

"It's worth a lot." Sam rubbed her hands together and looked around the cabin. "You talked to your dad, I take it."

"He talked to me, more like it . . . I still can't, well—ugh. I just can't believe he did that."

"If it helps any, he wasn't trying to start problems. I don't think he realized you hadn't told the sperm donor where you were."

"Sperm donor. Good one. That's what I call him too."

"You ever going to tell me the story there?"

"Probably not."

"Okay." It was funny. She'd come to Aisha's first, before going to Charlie's, to say one simple thing. Now that she was sitting across from her, however, it felt anything but. "So you're probably wondering why I'm here."

"Not really."

Sam raised an eyebrow.

"Probably for the same reason my dad was just here."

"No, I wasn't planning to tell you he'd spoken to Evan. I just wanted—"

"To tell me that you really care for my dad and you realize that might make me unhappy but you're adults and I'm basically one too, and you're going to pursue a relationship with each other and I just have to deal with it in a mature, self-controlled, supportive way—

just as you have tried to deal with some of my choices that you're less than happy with—although, really, that last bit can't apply as much to you as it does to him."

Charlie had already covered the tough subject! Joy danced through Sam's veins and made her heart spin a little, even as she smirked at Aisha's sardonic tone. "You and I really are genetically related, aren't we?"

Aisha's mouth quirked a little too. "So I'm told."

"Anyway, yes, that sort of was what I was going to say, but also . . ."

"Also what?" Aisha asked when Sam paused for too long.

"Well, I don't expect us to be bosom buddies or to take your real mom's place or anything, but, uh, if you didn't hate me, that would be nice."

"I don't . . . hate you. I was just angry, and I figured, since you were always planning to bolt first chance you got, I'd cut the cord first."

Sam looked down. Just say it, she told herself. Say it so it's out there once and for all, so we can both move on to . . . whatever, if anything, comes next. "I also wanted to tell you that while it might seem to you like I'm only here because I'm interested in Charlie, that's not the full story. Even if your dad and I had nothing between us, I would've turned around and come back tonight."

Aisha shrugged. "I know. You and Jo are tight. I was already schooling myself about how to deal with seeing you occasionally."

"No—that I'd still visit Jo is a given. I meant that I wouldn't just drop out of your and Mo's lives forever, or wouldn't unless you wanted me to. And regardless of your dad, I wanted to come back to extend an invitation—and a hope—that you and I could keep in touch." It was the truth, but Sam could see how it might seem self-serving.

Aisha didn't speak.

Sam got to her feet, her sore leg stiff from the drive, the rest of her rigid with unease. She had tried at least. "So, yeah . . . well, that's it. I'll go track down your old man now."

Aisha nodded and still didn't say anything—but she watched from the doorway to make sure Sam made it off the porch and down the stairs okay.

Sam was on the gravel, ready to start toward Rainbow, when Aisha's voice stopped her. "I just don't get it. Why does love have to hurt so much? Why does everything always have to end?"

Something in Sam's heart cracked and she wished she had some deep, comforting truth to impart, but even coming up empty she turned back. Aisha's crazy blond curls, backlit by the porch light, looked like a halo.

"I don't know, but I have learned something important recently."

Aisha crossed her arms over her chest. "Oh yeah? And what's that?"

"Sometimes not loving hurts more."

Aisha's eyes locked on hers and Sam held her gaze steadily, without faltering.

Finally Aisha nodded. "Hmpf. That's something my mom would've said."

Sam shrugged and adjusted her crutches. "What can I say? She sounds like a fount of wisdom and insight."

"Yeah, yeah." Aisha's dry tone held a hint of laughter, and she moved to shut the door.

"Wait." Sam raised her crutches. "Please, Aisha. I need to say what I actually came here to say. I'm sorry I keep avoiding it."

Aisha looked curious and kept the door open, but also didn't move closer to Sam.

"Do you mind if I sit down?" Sam asked.

Aisha shrugged and motioned at the porch's solitary rocking chair. Sam reclimbed the stairs and sat.

"Should I get us tea or something?" Aisha asked.

"That'd be great." And it was. Holding the hot mug was comforting and kept her rooted securely in the present as her mind fell to the insecure jumble of her past.

"I appreciate how you haven't pushed for information about your birth father. It's a lame, predictable story, I'm afraid—not a lot of drama or intrigue at all."

"Stop stalling," Aisha said, with a small grin.

Sam nodded. "I was a precocious kid and a nightmare of a teenager, or I would've been had anyone cared or tried to rein me in. When I was thirteen I hung out with boys with cars. When I was in high school I dated men."

Aisha made a face.

"Yeah," Sam agreed. "But there were good times too—and a lot of it was an act. I was a big talker mostly. For all my carefully projected worldliness I was brutally naïve in other ways. All I wanted was to belong. To have polish and money. To be special." Sam sipped her tea. "So, of course, I fell for a guy and a lie that gave me a false sense of those things."

"Close your eyes." But the voice wasn't Sam's. Wasn't Aisha's. It was his. *Rick's.* Hearing it again, even just in her head, made Sam's body burn with humiliation.

Sam had complied. The flickering candle on the table made her see red and gold undulating waves against her closed lids. Even now she remembered how, with her eyes closed, all her other senses were heightened. The flame's heat licked her face—then her hair lifted off her shoulders and a slightly damp mouth pressed against her exposed flesh. Rick's Polo cologne filled her nose and his smooth hands gripped her neck and squeezed lightly.

"Delicious," he murmured. A second later, something slippery slid over her skin. Her hand flew up to the slick beads circling her throat in two cold strands.

"Oh . . ."

"Pearls," Rick whispered.

Pearls? That made her smile. Jewelry like that was

the kind of present you bought a woman who meant something to you, like a wife, not just a piece of ass on the side. Which all went to show that Sam was right and her best friend Anna was wrong. And with a friend who said things like that about you, who needed enemies? Besides, she had Jo. She had Rick—and Rick's friends would eventually be her friends, too. It might be a little awkward at first, but they had to know what a bitch Lara was. Surely they'd want him to be with someone who loved him, who made him happy—

"Okay, open your eyes, babe."

Again, Sam did as she was told. Rick was holding a round silver mirror in front of her, gripping her hair in a loose topknot. Sam's eyes widened at her reflection. She'd never noticed before, but in this light, in this smoky room, with her hair up, she looked a lot like her mother.

Rick misunderstood her mild shock as delight, rested his chin on her shoulder, and grinned lasciviously at their double reflection. "Smoking," he hissed.

Sam felt a little ill. Looking at Rick head on, he was handsome and polished like some movie star or actor who played a lawyer on TV. In the mirror together, however, she not only looked like her mom, her boy toy of choice was old—too old—also like her mom's.

"They're really nice, thank you," she said.

Rick sat back down and Sam's composure returned. He was good looking. He was rich. And he saw all the qualities in her that she wanted to possess.

She pushed her doubts away and beamed while he ordered for her—drinks and everything and she didn't even get ID'd. She was already looking forward to the after dinner party. He was going to introduce her to some of his friends. That had to mean something, right?

"Ugh, you were an idiot." Aisha's sharp groan of disbelief cut into Sam's story, pulling her back to the porch and the dregs of her tea. She wrapped both hands around her mug. "Yeah, and you don't know the half of it."

"So it wasn't rape or anything like that?"

"Nope. Just pure stupidity, I'm afraid. That was the first night we had sex, and I was on the pill. . . . I just didn't know antibiotics I was taking for something else basically cancelled it out."

"So you got blitzed when I was pregnant?"

Sam winced. "A few times, but only before I found out. And you're fine."

"Does this Rick guy know I exist?"

Truth or lie, Sam pondered. She nodded slowly.

"And he didn't care?"

"No. Denied you were his, and a paternity test? Well, it wasn't even something that entered my head as a possibility."

"I don't mean to be rude, but are you positive it was him, not—"

"I'm sure. I was a vagina-virgin until I met him."

"A *what*? That's an awful thing to refer to anyone as."

"I'm sorry—and I'm sorry I don't have a nicer story to tell you about your conception, something involving young love or star-crossed but genuine lovers."

"Is that why you broke up, because of me?"

"Not even close. We carried on for a bit because I didn't know I was carrying you until I was almost four months in. It was something that happened later."

"What—or is that too personal?"

Sam smiled ruefully and shook her head. "This is your story too, for better or worse. Of course it's not too personal."

Aisha poured them more tea.

"We went to a small party—in a huge, fancy house up on the bench. It was held in this big rec room in the basement that had a leather bar counter and everything. I was young enough to think it was 'awesome' and 'cool,' not tackier than hell."

Aisha laughed, sounding a bit nervous to Sam.

"It took me a few minutes to realize something was strange—then I pinpointed it. I was the only girl at the party."

Aisha made a concerned noise.

"I know, right? Anyway, Rick took my jacket and within all of three minutes I knew I'd made a huge, stupid, embarrassing mistake." The heat in Sam's cheeks told her she was blushing again.

"As he took off my coat, he gave me a little spin. I was wearing a fitted white dress with a diamond shaped cut out in the front—hello, eighties!—that he'd bought for me. I smiled, feeling flattered, like we were dancing or something . . . and then he said, 'So what'd I tell you, guys? Can you believe it?'"

Aisha looked perplexed and Sam ran her finger along the rim of her mug. "It wasn't what he said so much as how he said it, his tone or something, and the way the men in the room looked at me. I . . . it was just . . . " Sam broke off, shaking her head.

"Anyway his oiliness there was just the cake. The *icing* on the cake was that at the same moment, a petite blonde—the guy who owned the house's wife, I found out later—came down the stairs with a huge tray of snacks."

And suddenly, just like that, Sam was back in that excruciating moment.

The woman's cool, penetrating eyes caught Sam's and she shook her head.

"Just a poker night with the guys, hey? No wives, but dates are all right? What is she, all of seventeen? You're disgusting." The woman had put the tray down on a counter and started back up the stairs when her husband hollered, "What's the problem, honey? You see the girl you used to be and feel a bit left out?"

Aisha made an exaggerated gagging sound.

Sam started. "Too much? I'm sorry."

"Not too much. I just feel a bit homicidal right

now."

Sam nodded.

"So that's when you figured it out, that you should end it, when you saw what a pig he was?"

Sam shook her head. "No, actually, it was the expression in the woman's eyes when she looked at me, sad. Sad and resigned." What Sam didn't say—and God-willing would go to her grave with—was who the woman was. Caren Archer. As in Callum's mother. It had given her a real turn when she'd shown up in Greenridge to deal with her Uncle's estate and she realized old Duncan was still around. She, of course, had flirted with him and acted like she didn't know him at all—just in the off chance he remembered her. Who wanted to look like some lame, taken advantage of kid?

Aisha was talking again and Sam pulled herself, with difficulty, back to the present once more.

"Have you ever married?"

"Nope. Came close a few times, but no cigar."

"Because your heart was broken?"

Sam was about to say yes, but then a nugget of truth choked her. Why hadn't she seen it before?

"Yes and no. My heart was broken long before I met creepy Rick. I think it was pride. I was so ashamed of being so dumb that I kept everyone at a distance after that. I never wanted to be that weak—or that humiliated again." Sam saw the expression in Aisha's eyes and attempted to lighten the mood with another truth. "Don't feel too badly for me. I've also had a lot of fun."

Aisha's eyes narrowed at Sam's grin. "Yeah, I'll bet."

A low gurgle and half cry came from the cabin. Aisha cocked her head, listening. Sam couldn't believe she'd practically forgotten little sleeping Mo. "Do you have to get her?"

Silence from the cracked door. "Not yet, but soon. I have one more question."

"Yeah?"

"Why'd you keep me if the situation surrounding my conception was so messed up?"

Sam smiled. "I guess, despite all my cynicism, I liked the idea of some Kendall girl living the good life somewhere."

Aisha snort-laughed. "Well, sorry to disappoint you."

Convoluted emotions made Sam's voice a little sharper than she intended. "Don't be ridiculous. I'm not disappointed at all. You're all I hoped you'd be and more."

Aisha blushed and laced and unlaced her fingers.

"Sam?"

"Yeah?"

"I still don't think you and my dad are a good idea. I'm sorry."

Sam laughed. "That makes two of us, but I'm not backing off. And *I'm* sorry about that."

In the cabin, Mo let out a blood-curdling scream.

"Alrighty then," Aisha said. Sam didn't know who triggered the comment: the baby or her.

But Aisha didn't disappear immediately. "Do you mind?" she asked.

Sam was confused at first. Then Aisha gave her a hesitant one-armed side hug. She wrapped her arm around Aisha's waist and squeezed back just as cautiously.

When Aisha stepped away, she nodded once and headed into the cabin. Sam waved a crutch at her daughter's retreating figure. Life was a surprising thing sometimes. And not always in a terrible way, either.

Chapter 29

DOG SPRANG TO HER SIDE from behind the cover of a nearby hedge as if to check where Sam was, making Sam giggle.

"I'm here. You're fine. Go play."

Dog bounded off with almost as much giddy joy as Sam was feeling. She leaned her crutches against the deck, gripped the handrail, and did a one-legged hop up the stairs, trying to be as quiet as she could so she wouldn't lose the element of surprise. It was no use though. The door whipped open before she made it across the porch.

"Sam." Charlie's voice was like hot chocolate or coffee with heavy cream, smooth and comforting, warming her from the inside out. "You came back."

"I did."

His eyes squinted in a smile and he held the door wide open to her.

"So you checked your phone messages I take it?"

Sam shook her head, accepting the arm he offered her for balance. Heat coursed through her at this simplest of physical connection. "Not yet. I wanted to know—and I wanted *you* to know—that I returned on my own volition because I decided I was being a twit."

"Hmm, sounds like you gave yourself quite a harsh lecture."

Sam laughed then sighed deeply as Charlie slid his arm around her waist and helped her to the couch. How could this silly cabin and this man feel so solidly like home after such a short time? She shook her head—then tuned into what Charlie was saying.

". . . so yeah, if you don't mind, I'd love it if you'd just delete those messages and spare me the humiliation."

"Say what?"

"They're . . . mortifying. Full of desperation and lovesick whining."

"Lovesick whining, hey?"

He bowed his head. "Yeah."

"Well, now you're talking. A full team of warriors couldn't keep me from listening to them."

Charlie settled onto the couch, tucked her against his side, and sighed softly.

"What?" Sam asked.

"Nothing—just that I've been so stupid."

"Oh, just that, hey? How so?"

"I actually thought I might not be up to loving you, that I couldn't handle the risk."

Sam laughed, earning a confused look from Charlie. "It just seems to be the theme of my life right now," she explained, and shot a look up to the ceiling. "I get it already. I get it."

"And?"

"And I agree, Charlie. There's nothing of value without risk."

He nodded. "I know it's early days, but I think . . . no, I know. I love you, Sam, and I want to see where our feelings take us. And if we fall out of love, I will never stop working until we fall back into it, and if you stop loving me, I'll love you—"

Sam put a finger to his mouth. "Is that the type of stuff your messages are full of?"

He winced. "Maybe."

She clapped. "Oh, goody. We can listen to them together, every night and—"

He grabbed her wrists and tugged her gently forward, then pressed his lips softly to hers, then harder.

Sam was dizzy in a lusty, blood surging sort of way when she pulled back. "Before we get too distracted— about what you were saying. That's how I feel too. It's sort of a miracle, isn't it?"

But Charlie's focus had moved on. "You think you can distract me?"

"Sweetie, I can frigging hypnotize you."

A low chuckle poured from Charlie's throat—then choked to a stop when Sam pressed her palm against his thigh, and ran her hand up. . . .

"I can't wait for you to give it your best shot," he murmured against her mouth.

Epilogue

RIVER'S SIGH WAS AN OASIS of every shade of green the mind could conjure—emerald and jade, evergreen and lime, moss and fern, you name it, and the flower-beds Jo had knocked herself out in all spring were a parade of joy and color. To heck with being a writer. Maybe he'd take up painting.

Charlie cut the engine and he and Sam climbed out of the Mercedes, accompanied by Dog who took off at a full run for Hoover who came out of the main house with Jo.

Sam headed for Jo right off too, and Charlie followed slowly, letting the rushing gurgle and sigh of the creek fill his senses with the peace every niche and cranny of the place seemed to offer. The sweet scent of nicotiana filled the early evening air but the bright blossoms weren't decked out any finer than Sam was, and the August sun was still hot and life giving—again, not unlike his new wife. His *wife*.

His phone beeped and Charlie read the incoming text from Theresa with a smile, then fired off a quick reply: "Great news, thanks. I'm stoked they like the two books and the new series idea. Just into River's Sigh. I'll call you tomorrow." He turned his phone off, shoved it into his pocket, and continued his trek, marveling again at his mind-blowing luck—and Sam's sweet ass—as he trailed behind her and Jo and the dogs down the path that led to Silver.

Dog ambled back to him and nudged his leg as if to say hurry up—and Sam looked back and winked like Dog was her private, psychically sent messenger.

"It's just so great—but also so surprising," Jo was saying. "You've only known each other six months."

Sam's laughter tinkled and cliché or not, Charlie felt like his heart might burst—and then Sam was replying. "Well, good grief, Jo—did you think I'd wait forever? We need to enjoy our S.B.S.G.B. ending, while we can."

Charlie caught up to the sister who held—and would always hold—his undying love and affection. Then he hugged her from behind. "Not a chance. There will be no stopping because there will be no shit that gets bad. We're definitely getting an H.E.A."

"A happily ever after, hey? For sure?"

"Yeah." He nuzzled her neck for emphasis. "*For sure.*"

Jo stepped away from them, laughing. "I have no idea what gibberish you guys are speaking, but if you're happy, I'm happy."

"I really am," Sam whispered.

"We both are," Charlie added, as Sam leaned into his body with a sigh.

"Oh, good grief, get a room," Jo said.

Sam winked. "Oh, we got one. Don't worry."

"Yeah," Charlie said. "And rumor has it that it sports a tub that fits two people just perfectly."

"I still can't believe you're the mysterious couple who rented Silver for all of August and into the fall," Jo said. "Or that Aisha actually managed to keep it a secret these past few weeks."

As if cued, Aisha appeared on Minnow's small porch, chubby little Mo perched on one hip. "I'll come visit after work," she hollered.

"Sounds good," they called back.

"Honestly, we just got married so we could honeymoon in that gorgeous tub," Sam said a moment later.

Jo smacked her. "Too much information. *Too much.*"

Sam laughed throatily. "It's too easy. I can't resist."

They were in front of Silver now and Charlie's head was filled with memories of the first time they'd shared the space together—how simultaneously tantalized and tortured he'd felt. A tremor of happiness and desire quaked through him. This time they'd share the space properly.

Sam crossed her arms over Charlie's and studied the posh cabin too. "And just think, once our new place is finished next door, neither you, Callum or the poor guy will ever be free of me."

"I'd better be the poor guy you mean," Charlie said.

"We'll see," Sam said coyly, and turned to face him. He loosened his hold on her just enough to accommodate the shift.

"Well, that's my cue." Jo placed the keys on Silver cabin's railing, whistled for Hoover, and sneaked away.

"Wait!" Sam called.

Jo turned back. "What's up?"

"On the phone, when I called to give you the heads up about when we'd get in, you said there's some big mess with your in-laws and Callum's black sheep of a brother is coming to River's Sigh for a visit?"

"Gag, don't remind me—and don't give it a thought. It's your honeymoon. Sufficient unto the day is the evil of the senior Archer men and all that. We'll talk later."

"Are you sure?"

Charlie held his breath. Of course he'd share Sam tonight if he had to, but that didn't mean he wanted to.

"I'm sure. Thanks though."

Sam waved and her full attention rested back on Charlie. He swooped her up and carried her over the threshold.

"I love you," she said after he settled her back on the ground and she stopped laughing. "No holds barred. No alternative route or exit plans. Thank you."

It was on the tip of Charlie's tongue to say I love you too, but he got confused. "What do you mean thank you?"

Sam shrugged, but didn't avert her eyes. "I . . . just never believed love would happen for me. I'm so grateful to you for showing me it exists in so many different ways."

"Well, you're welcome," Charlie said, his voice husky. "But from the moment you flipped me the bird on the highway, it never occurred to me that you wouldn't know how immensely loveable you are."

Sam laughed. "Uh huh."

"And not only do I love you today, Sam. I will love you for all of our days."

"Can I hold you to that?

"You'd better."

"I can't believe I ever thought I could do anything but love you," she said seriously. "I think I was waiting for you all of my life."

He kissed her. And then he kissed her again. And then he whispered, "Thank *you*."

Dear Reader,

I adored spending time with Sam and Charlie at River's Sigh B & B, my own dream getaway. If you enjoyed it too, you'll be happy to know their story—and the stories of so many other people living in or visiting Greenridge—continues in *Spoons*, Book 3 of the River's Sigh B & B series, coming Fall 2015.

I'd love to hear from you, so please visit **www.evbishop.com**, sign up for my newsletter, find me on Facebook or follow my Tweets (Ev_Bishop). And on a similar note, reviews really, really help authors. ☺ Please consider leaving a rating and a few kind words on Amazon, GoodReads, your blog, Facebook, or anywhere else you like to hang out when your nose isn't in a book. Thank you so much for reading.

Wishing you love, laughter and adventure—inside the pages and out of them,

Ev Bishop

Curious about Jo and Callum and the birth of River's Sigh B & B? For a peek at WEDDING BANDS, the story that started it all, read on. . . .

Prologue

The Past

JO SAT ON THE CHILLY metal bench under the grimy shelter in front of the bus station for as long as she could, kicking up gravel with the scuffed toes of her sneakers and drawing designs on the fogged up glass. Where was he, where was he, where was he?

She doodled her and Callum's names inside a heart-shaped flourish, then scrawled "True if erased!" beside it.

When she couldn't hold still any longer, Jo hopped to her feet and paced, not wanting to go inside the building because what if he arrived and thought she was the one who hadn't shown up? But it was raining harder now, and cold wind blew sheets of water into the shelter. She could care less if she was soaked to the skin usually, but the long bus ride would be uncomfortable if her jeans were soggy. Plus, she had to pee. Really bad.

She considered the cozy interior of the station—well, cozy by comparison to where she was now anyway—once more. Then looked up the street and down it. Callum's red Honda Civic was still nowhere to be seen. And anyway, he'd said he was going to walk. It was getting darker, but there were streetlights. She could see all too well there was no one walking toward her in any direction. She cracked her knuckles. The movement sparkled under the streetlight, and she looked down at the delicate gold band on her left ring finger. A tiny diamond twinkled up at her. She rubbed it with her thumb and grinned.

"Callum," she whispered. Then she laughed out loud. "Callum, hurry up!"

It boggled her mind that they were doing this. They were really doing this. They were running away to get married!

But at 9:30, Callum still hadn't shown up and the bus was supposed to board at 9:48. Jo's bottom lip had a raw groove in it from her teeth. A slow but steady trickle of people filed past her into the station to buy tickets, ship boxes, and say good-bye to departing family and friends. Jo's bladder moved past discomfort. It was going to burst. And her heart might too.

She headed into the station and beelined to the washroom. The stall was cramped but clean. She relieved herself without finding any real relief at all. Why hadn't he come? Where was he?

She made her way to the payphones on the back wall by the vending machines. Her sister Sam said one day people would have miniature phones they'd carry on them at all times to call people whenever they wanted. Jo always thought that was far-fetched. Who on earth had so many people to call that they couldn't wait till they got home? But tonight, picking up the gummy receiver, she changed her mind. Personal phones weren't a terrible idea. Maybe Sam was onto something.

Jo inserted her quarter and pressed each digit in Callum's phone number with utmost care, like she was performing a ritual or charm that would bring them together—or not.

The phone rang once, rang twice—was answered midway through the third ring by a clipped, impatient voice. "Yes?"

Rats. Mr. Archer. Callum's dad. He hated her.

"Um, hello, Mr. Archer?"

No acknowledgement that yes, it was him. Not even a grunt.

"Is Callum there, please?"

Mr. Archer's voice warmed suddenly. "Is this you Tracey?"

"Um, no—"

"Oh, I'm sorry. Selene?"

"No, I'm—"

A chuckle interrupted her. "Sorry, sorry. You know how it is for an old dad, trying to keep up with a young buck's does."

A young buck's does? Jo traced a crack in the tile with her toe. What a creep.

"It's Jo," she said, "Jo Kendall."

"Oh, sorry, lad—thought you were a girl for a minute. Must be a poor connection."

Jo exhaled. Her knuckles were white on the receiver. "We've met, Mr. Archer. I've been dating Callum all year."

"Oh, *oh . . .* " There was a shuffling sound, then a porcelain clank, like a plate dropped too quickly onto another. "Well, I don't keep track. He took off with someone in a blue Volkswagen about an hour ago. I just assumed the driver was the girl in his life these days. That's not you? Not your car?"

Jo bowed her head and mumbled into the mouthpiece, "No, not me. Thanks anyway. We'll probably all meet up at the same place later." She hoped she didn't sound as miserable as she felt. Who wanted to give the horrible man the satisfaction that she'd been ditched?

She hung the phone back in place, but stayed by the booth a moment, heels of her hands pressed into her eyes. What should she do? There was another bus at 5:30 a.m. Should she try to round Callum up? But on foot in the pouring rain in the growing darkness? She had no idea where to even start to look. Greenridge had a small population, sure, but it was scattered over a huge geographic area. At the very least, she should call Ray. Of course she should! Obviously Callum would've called to say he was held up. He wasn't an asshole.

Breathing easier, she dug for another quarter.

"Yeah-lo," a raspy voice answered.

Jo smiled at the familiar, corny combination of "Yeah and hello" her uncle always used.

"Hey, Uncle Ray. It's Jo. Has Callum called by any chance?"

"He sure did, kiddo. Sounded kinda upset. I took a message. Let me see. . . ."

Jo waited for Ray to rummage through his head for scraps of the conversation, a familiar, confusing mixture of love and irritation swirling in her gut. She prayed he hadn't hit the bottle too heavy already, or who knew what mixed up, incoherent babble he'd pass on.

But Ray didn't sound overly tipsy and wasn't slurring when he said, "Ah, here it is, princess."

Jo rolled her eyes. Her uncle was the only person in the world who looked at her and saw a princess.

"I wrote it down."

"Wow, will wonders never cease?" The words slipped out before she could stop them.

Uncle Ray only laughed. "Wait a minute, I thought you said you were Jo? How come you're sounding like your big sister Sam?"

Jo shifted from one foot to the other. It was 9:39. People streamed out of the small station toward the big Greyhound rumbling outside.

"He said, um . . . " Jo could practically see Ray squinting at his barely legible scrawl. "He's sorry, but it's over. It won't work—repeated that three times, angry-like. 'It won't work—just won't work.' Does that make any sense?"

Jo closed her eyes and squeezed the bridge of her nose. It made no sense. It also made perfect sense. She could hardly speak. "Yeah, yeah, it does. Thanks."

"Call me when you get settled back at your mom's, all right?"

Jo forced a few more words out. "Yes, yes, I will."

"I love you, baby girl."

The words coaxed a blurry-eyed smile. Oh, Uncle Ray. "I love you too." And she did, but like everything in her life, it was so damned complicated. How could you love someone and not really ever be there for them? Never get your shit together? You'd think with her history, Jo would be used to it by now, but she wasn't. Some day she was going to have a home. A real one. A non-temporary, longer than a summer or a school year place to stay. She and Callum both wanted that—or then again, maybe not. Maybe just she did. She alone. Again.

She swallowed hard and stared up at the ceiling, willing the tide of saltwater in her eyes to recede. She pressed a hand to her sickish-feeling stomach. What was she going to do?

A crackly voice came over the P.A. system and announced last call for eastbound travellers.

Her suitcase was already stowed in the belly of the bus, loaded while she'd sat around waiting. It would be hard to change her mind now, even if she wanted to—

and did she want to? Did she want to wander around the small town all summer, facing memories of Callum everywhere? Did she want to have some big high-drama face off with him about the how and why of him calling everything off so randomly and so last minute? No, she just couldn't. It was too hard. And Ray's, much as she loved him, wasn't the place for her anymore. Things were going from bad to worse for him—and she'd just turned eighteen, just graduated. She was too young to settle down to take care of her uncle who was drinking himself to death and refused help. Even through the pain, she knew that.

She took a deep breath, hoisted her backpack, then limped outside as if physically injured. It felt like she was. On her way toward the silver-haired bus driver who stood by the bus door collecting tickets, she passed by the shelter. The blurred words "Callum + Jo, forever. True if erased!" jumped off the glass at her. Out of habit, she lifted her hand to rub the words away, then realized how dumb she was. Her hand returned to her queasy stomach. She boarded the bus.

Chapter 1

The Present

THE EVENING AIR WAS CRISP but not yet freezing. Jo stopped in her tracks just to inhale. The comforting scent of cedar smoke from the house's chimney, the salty-sweet smell of smoking salmon, and the earthy fragrance of the changing season thrilled through her. She wanted to pinch herself. It was all really hers— well, *theirs*. Her sister Samantha would see the light eventually. Imagine living here all year round. It would be like a postcard every season. All the work was worth it. How could Samantha want to get rid of this place? Was she crazy?

The first fallen leaves gleamed gold against the dark lawn and crackled under her boots as she continued toward the old house. The porch light glowed a friendly welcome, though its beam created shadows around her that she wouldn't have noticed if there'd been no light at all.

Jo climbed the three steps to the home's wraparound porch, and leaned her trout rod against a wall, well out of the way of the door. She was careful to make sure the pretty—and more importantly, lucky—wedding band lure, a bright beaded thing encrusted with rhinestones, was safely held in one of the rod's eyes. She tucked her tackle box beside the rod and carried her basket of treasure into the house. Fresh caught Rainbows—even their name was gorgeous. She whispered a prayer of thanks for the beauty and bounty of the area. Her stomach rumbled.

Jo whistled for Hoover, but the dog didn't come. He was probably still by the river, roaming about. She crossed her fingers that he hadn't found something disgusting to roll in—his favorite trick—and whistled again. Still nothing. Used to his selective hearing and even more selective obedience, she happily transitioned to thoughts of side dishes. Asparagus and oven-roasted baby potatoes? Rice pilaf and broccoli rabe? Mmmm.

She kicked off her rubber boots and left them where they fell. Yes, they blocked the door, but wasn't that one of the luxuries of living alone? The time would come soon enough when she had to worry about appearances and keeping everything just so. She imagined a houseful of paying guests and smiled.

She left her old black and red checked flannel jacket on. She'd get the fish frying before she cleaned up.

Halfway down the darkened hall toward the kitchen, Jo's stomach tightened. There was a light on—and she knew she'd turned them all off.

"Hello?" she called, and felt stupid when she realized she'd clutched the buck knife attached to her belt. What was she going to do? Stab an intruder?

"Hello," she said again, louder.

The voice that answered almost stopped her heart.

"Jo—is that you, finally? I've been waiting all night. Where were you?"

Jo relaxed her grip on the knife handle reluctantly. If there was someone she actually wouldn't mind stabbing it would be—

"Come on, don't you have a kiss for your sis?"

—Yep, her "sis." Samantha.

Jo flipped a switch, and another feeble bulb lit up. It didn't do much to brighten the wood panel hall, but would keep Jo from colliding with Sam—or colliding literally, anyway. That was the first of many things Samantha complained about regarding the cabin they'd inherited from their uncle: its "archaic" lighting.

Samantha's high heels clacked across the hardwood floor in the living room, then moved into the kitchen. Jo cringed, envisioning the dints she was probably leaving in her wake.

"Good grief, Jo. It's a tomb in here. How do you stand it?"

Had she called it or what? "Every bulb doesn't have to glare. I like soft—"

"What's in the basket?"

How Jo wished she could disappear into one of the bedrooms, any one of them, no matter how cluttered or unfinished. But as she knew from a lifetime of experience, it wouldn't help. Samantha would be there, in her face, until she tired of chewing at whatever she was after this time—and since "this time" involved money, she wouldn't drop the bone till the cash was in hand.

"Trout," Jo admitted miserably, all fantasies of a candlelit dinner for one dashed to hell.

"Gross."

Jo shrugged. If only that opinion meant Samantha was planning to eat elsewhere—but Jo knew better than that. She headed for the counter beneath the big window that had a gorgeous mountain view, and dumped her catch into one of the stainless steel sinks. "Dot's doing Italian specials all week."

"Pasta? Like I'd eat pasta. Goes straight to your belly."

Jo patted her own "belly" with affection, not caring if she got fish slime on her shirt. It was due for a wash. "Well, I'm making potatoes."

Samantha followed her, keeping a safe three-foot distance from any potential food mess. She gave Jo a quick once over and frowned.

"What are you wearing? You stink like fresh air and you look like a lumberjack. And tonight of all nights!"

"What do you mean 'tonight'? What's so special about *tonight*?"

Jo scrubbed her hands and started peeling potatoes. Samantha sighed dramatically. "I was hoping you'd look human when you met my lawyer, but thankfully I've already warned him about you."

"Your *what*? Here, now—*what?*"

Samantha flourished one hand. "Callum, we're ready for you." A shadow moved in the dining room.

Crap.

Jo was so angry she could hardly see.

And then she was so startled she almost sliced her thumb with the potato peeler. She put it down. *Callum?* As in Callum Archer? Her old Callum? No . . . the first name was a coincidence. Had to be. A tall man walked out of the living room and extended his hand.

"Callum Archer," Samantha said and Jo's brain swam. "Josephine—or Jo, as she's sometimes called—my sister."

Jo tried to give the hand gripping hers a firm shake, but as she met his piercing aqua blue eyes—eyes she'd never forget—she started to freak out. An irrational observation hit her: the man, Sam's lawyer, *her old Callum*, had strong sexy-rough hands for a guy working a desk job. Her stomach churned. Breathe, she commanded herself. *Breathe.* It was absolutely no comfort at all that he looked as shocked as she felt.

"Hello Callum," she said, hoping desperately for a dry, casual tone. "It's been a long time." And it had been. Fifteen years, four months. Not that she'd counted. . . .

"*Jo*? I'll be damned." And Callum did look like he'd just been damned. All the blood drained from his already fair skin, making his blue eyes burn even brighter and his black hair seem all the blacker. "You look exactly the same," he said.

"When it's half dark, perhaps," Jo said wryly. "But thanks." So he was still a flatterer. That much hadn't changed.

Samantha's eagle sharp gaze darted to Callum, then speared Jo. "So what—you guys know each other?"

Jo raised her eyebrows and shook her head. "Uh, no. I wouldn't say that really. Used to. A bit. Kind of."

"Kind of," Callum repeated with a bitter note in his voice that Jo didn't understand—and that pissed her off. What the hell did he have to be bitter about?

There was a moment of uneasy silence, then Callum had the nerve to laugh. "Sisters. Wow." Jo hated the sexy, low timber of his voice and his easy confidence. "Here I'd just assumed the Josephine Kendall everyone in town was talking about, and that you went on about, was some aunt or something. I didn't link *Jo* to Josephine at all."

"Well, it's a terrible name, but it's better than *Jo*," Samantha said.

"She doesn't really strike me as the next thing to a bag lady," Callum said, his head tilting as he studied Jo.

The next thing to a bag lady? What on earth had Sam been telling people?

Samantha sounded as affronted as Jo felt. "Have

289

you taken a good look at her?"

Callum was still gripping Jo's hand and she yanked away, suddenly conscious of her muddy jeans, old man's shirt, and—no doubt—leaf and branch strewn hair. Shit. She was making an excellent first impression as a business professional, able to single-handedly turn the old cabin and overgrown property into a successful bed-and-breakfast, wasn't she? She could practically hear Samantha's victory chant.

She tried to fight the heat rising to her cheeks but failed, imagining how the room looked from his eyes. Breakfast and lunch dishes piled messily by the sink. A mishmash of junk littering the floor by the dishwasher. . . . She'd meant to box it up for Goodwill, but the beautiful fall afternoon had called to her. And what kind of ignoramus shows up unannounced and basically breaks into someone's house anyway?

"I'm not sure what my sister told you, or why either of you thought an impromptu, unscheduled appointment would be at all appropriate or beneficial"—she glared at Samantha for a moment—"but it's neither of those things. It's a Friday night, and I have plans. We can set up a time next week to meet at your office to discuss the estate and terms of my uncle's will, or, if you're from out of town, we can conference call."

Oh-so-confident Callum looked startled, and Jo made a couple more observations, all equally irritating. Time had been more than kind to him. While she'd found him gorgeous, like a rock god or something, back in the day—his tall, lanky frame had filled out with age. He looked more like a professional athlete than what her mind conjured for a lawyer. His icy blue eyes were still penetrating—and stood out spectacularly against his shock of silky raven hair—but he had just the start of crinkling laugh lines that softened his intensity. And he smelled good. Like fresh baked cookies, vanilla, cinnamon—

Callum's voice, sharp and irritated, cut through the buttery attraction melting through Jo. "You didn't arrange this? We just surprised her?" he said to Samantha.

Samantha waved her hand dismissively, and Jo wished she could lop one of those constantly gesturing hands right off. "She would've stalled indefinitely. And she doesn't really have plans. She's having dinner *by herself.*"

Like it's a capital crime or something, Jo thought.

Callum cleared his throat. "Sounds nice, actually. I'm sorry for the misunderstanding—sorry we disturbed you."

Jo didn't lie and say it was fine. She herded them to the door.

"I don't know why you're being like this. We need to talk, get this figured out, decide what works best for everyone."

"We have talked, Samantha. We disagree on what 'works best' means. Your lawyer may call me next week, anytime Monday through Friday between nine and five. I'll consult my schedule and we can set an appointment."

"Your *schedule*?" Samantha mocked.

Callum placed a hand low on Samantha's back and guided her toward the door. "She's right, Samantha. This wasn't the right way to proceed."

"And just so you're aware. If you break into my house again, I'll call the cops and press charges."

Callum turned back from the door. "I'm not sure it's so simple as 'your' house, Jo—but again, my apologies for the intrusion. It was a misunderstanding. I'll be in touch."

"Jo—"

"Let's just go, Samantha."

"Yes, *go,* Samantha. Take your slimy lawyer's advice. That's what you're paying him for right?"

Jo leaned against the mudroom's wall after they left and closed her eyes. Why had she been so rude? Yes, even after all these years, the very thought of Callum was a slicing barb—but that was no excuse. They'd been kids. She needed to let him off the hook. For her own sake, not just his.

What's next for Callum and Jo? Read WEDDING BANDS, Book 1 in the River's Sigh B & B series today.

About Ev Bishop

 **Ev Bishop** is a longtime columnist with the *Terrace Standard,* and her other non-fiction articles and essays have been published across North America. Her true love, however, is fiction, and she writes in a variety of lengths and genres. If you're a short story lover or read other genres alongside romance, visit www.evbishop.com to learn more.

Some short story publications include: "Not All Magic is Nice," *Pulp Literature*, "The Picture Book," *Every Day Fiction Magazine*, "Riddles," *100 Stories for Queensland,* "On the Wall," *Every Day Fiction Magazine,* "My Mom is a Freak," *Cleavage: Breakaway Fiction for Real Girls*, "HVS," "Red Bird," and "Wishful," (available through Ether Books).

Novels include *Bigger Things*, *Wedding Bands*, Book 1 in the River's Sigh B & B series, and *Spoons*, Book 3 in the River's Sigh B & B series (forthcoming). She also writes romance under the pen name Toni Sheridan (*The Present* and *Drummer Boy*).